LOOKING BACK:
A Boy's Civil War Memories

LOOKING BACK:
A Boy's Civil War Memories
★ ★ ★

GERALDINE LEE SUSI

E.M. Press, Inc.
Warrenton, VA

LOOKING BACK
This novel is a work of fiction. With the exception of historical figures, all characters in this novel are fictitious. Any resemblance to living persons, present or past, is coincidental.

Copyright © 2001 by Geraldine Lee Susi
All rights reserved. No part of this book may be reproduced or utilized in any form or by any means, electronic or mechanical, including photocopying, or by any information storage and retrieval system without permission in writing from the publisher.

Cover design by Lori Susi.
Illustrations by Geraldine Lee Susi.

E.M. Press, Inc.
P.O. Box 336
Warrenton, VA 20188

RL: 4.5
   Library of Congress Cataloging-in-Publication Data

Susi, Geraldine Lee.
  Looking back: a boy's Civil War memories / Geraldine Lee Susi.
     p. cm.
  Sequel to: Looking for Pa.
  Summary: In April of 1865, fifteen-year-old Jacob is captured and imprisoned as a Rebel soldier and spends his captivity remembering how the last four years of the Civil War have changed his peaceful life in Virginia.
    ISBN 1-880664-34-8 (alk. paper)
     1. Virginia--History--Civil War, 1861-1865--Juvenile fiction. [1. Virginia--History--Civil War, 1861-1865--Fiction. 2. United States--History--Civil War, 1861-1865--Fiction.] I. Title.

PZ7.S96565 Lm 2001
[Fic]--dc21   2001033484

To my husband,
Ron,
who supports all my endeavors, no matter how complicated,
who shares all my dreams, no matter how wild,
but, most of all,
who is my best friend in the whole wide world.

To my Mum and
who ...

Acknowledgements

To all of my friends
who read each draft and offered advice,
suggestions and encouragement,
thank you.

To Dave Purschwitz,
Manassas Museum curator,
who shared his expertise about the 8th Infantry
and provided other invaluable research assistance,
many, many thanks.

And finally,
to Carolyn Tuttle,
my high school English teacher and dear friend,
a special thank you.
Although she is no longer with us,
she spent her 89 years making this world a better place.
I will miss her guidance on all my future endeavors.

1
Capture at Sayler's Creek, April 6, 1865

"Pa! Conor!" I gasped. "Wait for me!" But I realized that they couldn't hear me. I couldn't even see them anymore. The slick red mud grabbed at my worn-out boots, sucking them into the cold wet ground. Thorny briar branches clawed at my arms and my clothes, slowing my escape at every turn. Still, I thought, I can catch up, and then I tripped over a root and fell face first into the muck. My rifle flew out of my hands and landed a few feet in front of me. As I lay there gasping for breath, I heard footsteps coming up behind me. Crawling through the slippery clay, I tried desperately to get to my gun. Too late!

"Stop where you are! Don't move!"

On my hands and knees, and covered with cold, wet mud, I couldn't see who was yelling, but within seconds, I felt the hard barrel of a rifle shoved between my shoulder blades. Shivers raced up and down my spine, and a sick feeling in my stomach moved up to my throat.

"Stand up slowly, and put your hands in the air," the voice ordered. "Don't move until I tell you to."

I could hear rustling behind me, and then the soldier moved into my sight as he picked up my gun. The sight of his blue Union uniform and the barrel of a gun aimed directly at me sent new waves of fear through my whole being. I knew from the minute I heard his command that what I feared most was a certainty. I had been captured. I was a Yankee prisoner. The cold, the exhaustion, and the hunger that had been with me for days now overwhelmed me. My legs began to tremble so violently that I wasn't sure they would support me.

★ ★ ★

"Turn around, Reb, and start walking. We've rounded up a bunch of you graybacks today, and the whole lot of you will probably sit out the rest of this war at Point Lookout Prison. We're just gonna keep whittling you down until you have to give up."

As I forced my feet to move as ordered, I dared to take one final glance in the direction that I'd last seen Pa and Conor heading. I didn't really know if I were hoping that one of them might be there to rescue me, or if I just wanted to catch sight of them still free and heading west to Appomattox to meet up with General Lee's forces. But there was no one to be seen. I was alone in enemy hands.

"Eyes forward, Reb, and start marching. I ain't got all day."

Ashamed and defeated, I slumped off in the direction the Yank indicated, willing my legs to make each torturous step.

2
Our Lives Change Forever

My name is Jacob, Jacob Harding. I'm fifteen. I'll be sixteen in September, if I live that long. Catlett, Virginia, is my home, or at least it was when this whole war began. Right now I don't know where home is. All I do know is that the fighting and the killing that has taken place over the last four years has changed my life in so many ways. It has, in fact, changed everything that's important to me. My family, my farm, even my country. Now I'm beginning to wonder if any of these will be there at all when I get out of this predicament. That is, of course, *if* I ever get out of here.

★ ★ ★

What began five years ago as an act of defiance among the southern states, has turned our whole land into killing fields. Virginia, my Virginia, has been nearly destroyed by all the fighting that has taken place on our once peaceful, rolling green hills. I've hated this war from the beginning, for what it has done to everyone and everything around me. I never wanted to be a part of it, of this "war of aggression," this "unpleasantness," or whatever names people want to call it. Yet somehow, even I found myself swept away by the current of emotions that seemed to catch up everyone and everything in its path. I still find myself trying to figure out how it all got so out of hand and, even more, how I let myself get drawn into this whole mess. Now, as I march forward into the midst of my enemies, I wonder if I, if we, could have avoided any of this. Somehow it always seems easier to look back, look back and see how things might have been different.

*　*　*

I was born on our farm in Catlett. It wasn't big, but it provided everything we needed, everything we wanted. My father and mother, Nathan and Annie Harding, had worked hard to make a good life for us. They had long ago struck out on their own, determined to make a life for themselves relying only on each other. They carved out a small, secluded farm shielded by stands of hickory, oak, and pine trees in the fertile farmlands of Fauquier County. I was their first child born in the small cabin they had built together. Two more baby boys followed, but neither one lived more than a few months. I don't remember either of them, but I know it was a difficult

★　★　★

time for Ma and Pa because there was little anyone could do if a baby wasn't strong enough to survive. Then my sister, Jessie, was born when I was three. She was not only a strong baby, but a happy one as well. She made us all laugh and smile. Jessie and I grew up not only as brother and sister, but, better yet, as best friends. From our parents we learned about love and loyalty, and we were content to exist together in our own little world. I've wondered if things might have continued that way forever if the war hadn't changed everything. Though I'm sure change would have come sooner or later, I guess we just never figured it would come as it did. For us it all really began to happen in April of 1861. That seems so long ago now. But I guess that really was when we first learned of the events that would change our lives forever.

3
Alarming News, April, 1861

While on one of his supply trips to Warrenton, Pa came back with some alarming news. Our state convention had voted in favor of secession, and as a result, the Governor was calling for volunteers to protect Virginia from Federal aggression. Pa told me that he was going to sign on with the Army of the Confederate States. He said it was something he felt he had to do. He believed that the Union was a threat to farmers and their way of life, especially in Virginia. Other states in the South felt the same way and had already taken steps to withdraw from the Union. They had formed the Confederated States of America. Naturally they would understand

★ ★ ★

the needs of the Southern farmers, and so Pa was willing to pledge to fight for them if necessary. He and everyone else was convinced that this disagreement would be over quickly. The South would go its separate way and everything could return to life as usual.

A few days after that, Pa took me aside and tried to explain what was happening in a way that I would understand.

"Jacob, let's go sit under the hickory tree. I need to explain a lot of things to you in a short time, boy, and I hope you can understand."

"Sure, Pa. You know I can do anythin' you ask me to do. An' you know I do my best. I try mighty hard."

"I know you do, son, and that's why I know I can do what I gotta do, and I know I can trust you to take care of things."

"Sure, Pa."

"Sit down, boy. I'll try to explain what's going on and what your Pa intends to do about it." Pa had paused and I remember waiting for him to begin again.

★ ★ ★

"Son, I know you've heard me talkin' to your ma about the things that have been goin' on in the South throughout this winter. South Carolina upped and left the Union and President Lincoln ain't been takin' too kindly to all that's been happenin'. Six more states joined up with South Carolina and they elected Mr. Jefferson Davis to be their president. Now I thought maybe our Virginia could stay out of all this fuss and that maybe Mr. Lincoln would just leave things alone. Even our own Governor Letcher tried to set up a peace convention here in the state. It almost worked. That was until Mr. Lincoln declared war in the middle of April and called for 75,000 soldiers to put down those states that were causin' the uprisin'. Virginia had to take a stand. What I found out in town was that on April 17th, our state delegates voted to secede from the Union. So now Virginia's taken a stand with the South. Governor Letcher's callin' for volunteers to fight with the Southern armies. Volunteers to defend our state, our liberties, and our homes. Son, we're farmers and we ain't got much, but we got to fight for what's right and what we believe in. We ain't got industry like the North. Farmin's all I know and I want to keep Virginia the way it is. A lot of other Virginians from this northern part are torn about what to do. There were lots of hard words and hard feelin's in town. But I told your ma the other night that I'm goin' to go an' enlist. I'll help you get everythin' in order before I go, but they need men now. Your ma's strong and she understands. She don't like it none, but she knows I gotta do this. You and Jessie can help keep things goin' while I'm gone. You been helpin' me since you was old enough to follow along behind a plow. I know you'll be all right until I get back. The way folks is

★ ★ ★

talkin', this ain't goin' to take long. I'll be back before the crops are ready to come in."

"But, Pa, why have you got to go? Ain't there enough other men that ain't got families?"

"Son, it don't work that way. A man has to do what he thinks is right and important. I can't set around hopin' someone else will fight my battles for me. You remember that, boy. If it's important to you, then you gotta fight for it. The way we live is important to me. I want it to stay this way. Do you understand what I'm sayin' to you, boy?"

"I think so, Pa. But I'm afraid what might happen—what might happen to you. Will it be dangerous, Pa?"

"Whenever men get to shootin' at one another it's dangerous. But maybe it won't have to come to that. We Hardings know how to take care of ourselves. That's why I tried to teach you everythin' I could as soon as you could learn it. You've been the best right-hand man a father could have, and that's why I know I can trust you to take care of the farm and help your ma. I've always said, us Hardings don't need nobody else. We take care of our own. We ain't beholden to nobody for nothin'. We work hard or we trade for all we got. You remember that, too, boy. We're proud folk. We ain't got much, but we got enough to be healthy and happy. We don't ever beg for nothin'. You got that, boy?"

I remember nodding my head in agreement, but as I look back now, I realize how little I really understood at that moment.

4
Man of the Family, May, 1861

The following month, Nathan Harding left us behind and

★ ★ ★

LOOKING BACK

★ ★ ★

joined up with the 8th Virginia Infantry, Company B. I was eleven years old, and I was to be the man of the family. Along with Ma and my eight-year-old sister, Jessie, the three of us would work the farm until he returned. We all stood and watched as Pa rode off so proud and tall on Dramus, the family mule. Again he assured us that he would be home before the crops came in. And we had no reason to doubt his words. But none of us ever suspected what lay ahead. Not me, not Jessie, and, especially, not Ma. That's always the most difficult memory for me. I will always feel somehow responsible for what happened to her, in spite of everyone's reassurances to me since then. I know now that there was little I could have done differently.

After Pa left us, we worked together like we always did. Daily chores were done, the garden tended to, and the animals cared for. Then one day Ma got sick. At first it didn't seem to be more than a bad spring cold that she'd caught after getting drenched in an unexpected rainstorm. While Ma rested in the house, Jessie and I continued with the farm chores as well as taking care of her. We'd always worked in the fields and in the house, so we just worked harder, doing Pa's work and Ma's, too. But as days went by, Ma got weaker and weaker. She didn't seem to have the strength to fight off the sickness, which eventually laid her up in bed. I didn't know what to do to help her. I can still see her pale face, her hair damp with sweat, as I sat beside her that last night. Those terrible rattling sounds that came when her breathing was so difficult had stopped. I remember dozing off thinking she was just sleeping peacefully. When I woke the next morning, I realized that she was too quiet, too peaceful. It was during

★ ★ ★

that night that she left us forever. That was July 7, 1861, a night I will always remember with the greatest of sadness.

Jessie and I buried Ma up on the little hill beside the graves of the two baby brothers we had never known. It was the most difficult thing either of us had ever done in our lives. And it would remain etched in our minds forever.

Facing such tremendous loss and not knowing where to turn, we decided that we had to go find Pa. He needed to know what had happened to Ma. We were sure that he would be able to come back to the farm with us. How naive we were! Jessie and I had no idea then what it meant to enlist as a soldier. Of course, at that point in time, there had been no fighting, no battles, no killing, so why shouldn't our father come back to his farm, back to what he'd always done, and be with us when we needed him more than the Army did?

Why, we even thought it would only take us a day or two to find him. We took along Nanny, our goat, Squealer, our pig, and our kitten named Cat since there would be no one left to feed or care for them. That was a good decision because that search ended up taking us more than two weeks and brought us right up to the brink of the war.

5
Looking for Pa, July, 1861

Jessie and I never imagined the many directions that journey would take us. For two children who had been sheltered in the safety of their family farm, we experienced and learned a lot during those two weeks. Poor Jessie! She has had to endure so much over these past four years. Maybe someday

★ ★ ★

I'll be able to make it up to her. Thinking of her and home makes me realize that I can endure anything if it means getting back to my family again.

Jessie was a plucky eight-year-old then, and she'd done all right as we searched for Pa. We met some nice folks, and we met some who were not so nice. Ol' Vergil Turner, for instance, was the meanest man we ever set eyes on. When he offered to take us to Rectortown in his wagon, we had no idea he never intended to get us there. We just thought he was being neighborly. Instead, he took us to his rundown shack, and I still don't know how long he would have kept us there if we hadn't figured a way to get out and run away. Thank goodness, Nanny applied her strong goat horns to Vergil's backside and helped us escape that day.

Then there was the powerful thunderstorm that caught us by surprise. Jessie and I ducked under a bridge to get out of the pouring rain. Before we knew what had happened, a raging torrent of water raced through the creek bed. I got tangled up in Squealer's rope, and we were swept away into the swirling muddy waters. All that had kept me afloat was holding onto the pig's fat, roly-poly body. If it hadn't been for a fallen log lying across the flooded stream, both of us would surely have drowned. Luckily, I was able to catch hold of it and pull myself and the pig out of the raging waters.

Squealer, however, seemed destined for trouble. Just a few days later came his fateful meeting with a family of bears. Only a somewhat stupid and very greedy pig would ever get between a mother bear and her cub, and all over a few rotting peaches on the ground. When the sound of growling woke me and Jessie that morning, we made a mad dash to get away

★ ★ ★

from the bears. When we finally dared to come back to collect our belongings, all that we found of the pig was Squealer's blood-stained rope. We were sure that we would never see him again.

There were also good and kind people that we met. Like John Lanham at Salem Station. He was a gentle old man whose son, it turned out, was fighting in Pa's unit. John fed us, gave us a place to stay for the night and helped us find out where Pa's unit might be headed so we could find him. Fortunately for us, John would remain our friend as time went on.

When we finally got to Bull Run where we hoped to find Pa, we made the acquaintance of James Robinson, a kind freedman. A former slave who had been given his freedom, Jim was also a very special friend. It is hard for me to think that Jim had once been someone's property. He helped me and Jessie and Pa in so many ways. Jim had explained to me how he had worked hard ever since he had been given his freedom in order to save money so he could try to buy his wife and children out of slavery. As the war went on, many of the Yankees said that was what they were fighting for, fighting to free the slaves. We never owned or used any slaves, so I couldn't understand that. But learning about Jim and his family left me even more confused about where this war and this fighting was taking us. Owning a man did not seem right to me, but then most folks I knew weren't fighting about that. They were fighting to protect their farms and their families from this Northern aggression. I certainly would not deny Jim's right to freedom. He was such a kind man. He was the one who finally found out where Pa's unit was, and in doing so realized that the fighting was probably going to end up

★ ★ ★

right in his backyard. He worried about losing everything he had worked so hard for all those years. He was determined to save his family and Jessie by making them hide down in the root cellar.

But I did not want to hide. If I hid I'd never find Pa. So I ran off and crouched down behind Jim's rail fence. I knew that Pa's unit, the 8th Virginia, would be out there somewhere, and I wasn't going to miss this chance to find him.

6
First Battle of Manassas, July 21, 1861

I remember that day so well. The soldiers appearing on that hill as if from everywhere. Uniforms and flags of gray, blue, red, and white were a kaleidoscope of colors on the field. That day it was impossible to tell who was Confederate and who was Union since many wore similar colors. Following that battle, both armies realized the importance of having distinct uniforms and distinct flags. Dark Yankee blue and dusty Rebel gray made it much easier to distinguish who was friend and who was foe after that. Bayonets glistened in the sun and the drummers beat a steady rhythm that echoed in my head. Roaring cannons reverberated in my stomach and resounding cracks of rifles came from every direction. Dying horses with their riders moaning in the blistering sun and the screams of each new rank of soldiers added to the cacophony that was deafening to my ears.

The noise was overwhelming, but it was at that moment that I saw a familiar head of curly blond hair moving forward across the hill. I knew it was Pa! I was going to yell out to

★ ★ ★

him when I saw him pitch backward with his arms out, his gun falling from his hands. And I watched as my Pa crumpled to the ground.

The only thing I thought about was getting to Pa lying there on the field. I leapt over the fence and raced toward him. It was like I was running on air. I felt a dull thud in my head and heard ringing in my ears. I remembered feeling like I was in slow motion. I just couldn't move any faster. My legs were moving as fast as they could go, but I couldn't seem to get to Pa. When I finally did, there was blood all over the front of Pa's jacket and I thought I was going to be sick. They were still shooting all around me. I took off my shirt and wadded it up. I pushed it inside Pa's jacket and held it against the wound to try to stop the bleeding. I thought I could feel his heart beat, but I wasn't sure. It was hard to tell. I remember wanting to yell to him, "Pa! Pa! You can't die. We need you. Jessie and me, we need you." But the noise of the battlefield drowned out everything. When I looked around, the soldiers were going back up the hill again. Retreating. The cannons were as loud as ever. I was afraid to cry out because I thought they might shoot me or Pa. I held my hand against the wound until it was numb. Just when I began to think the day would never end, bugles rang out again and soldiers surged forward once more toward the turnpike and the stone house. They were screaming out the Rebel yell. They were coming from everywhere and racing past me. Commanders on horseback charged and led the way across the ridge, and the gunfire seemed to move further away. I could see men running down the road, running down the turnpike towards the stone bridge. And I knew it must be over.

★ ★ ★

Finally I saw several Confederate soldiers coming across the field and I called out to them to help us. Lifting Pa onto their cart, they realized I had been wounded, too. I remembered putting my hand to my head and it was covered with blood. It was only a nick. But Pa's wounds were much more serious. They carried him away to one of the field hospitals that had been set up all along Bull Run following that battle.

7
After the Battle

Throughout the next few days, I stayed beside my father. Jessie remained with the Robinson family. They had been very lucky, for even with the cannons, minie balls, and fighting raging all around their home, there had been no damage. Just across the field, their neighbor, Mrs. Henry, had been much less fortunate. A mis-aimed cannon shot had not only destroyed her house, but had also cost the old woman her life.

The days right after the battle were very difficult. So many men from both armies lay lifeless across the hillsides. Soldiers from each side who were not needed with their units, stayed behind to bury their dead in shallow graves. The Union forces had retreated in such haste that many of their troops were left unaided. A Union hospital of sorts had been set up in the Matthew's stone house where Jessie and I had stayed only a few days before. Our Confederate wounded were cared for in field hospitals set up in tents and in other nearby homes and barns. My pa was in one of these. Eventually they moved

★ ★ ★

LOOKING BACK 17

as many of the wounded as they could by train to the hospital in Culpeper, and the rest were taken to Warrenton where they were cared for in schools and churches. The lucky Confederates were the ones who lived close enough to go to their own homes to recuperate. Home. As soon as Pa was strong enough to travel, that's where I took him.

While Pa was being cared for, the rest of his 8th Virginia unit rushed down the road to Manassas Junction to protect the railroad from a Union attack. The railroads that converged at the junction were the main reason for the Confederate success in that first battle. It was by rail that Jackson's and Beauregard's reinforcements had come in to provide the extra men that the South needed to win the battle on July 21st. Control of those railroads would be important throughout the war.

Two days later, the 8th came back through the battlefield on their way to Leesburg to guard the outposts along the Potomac River. Several members of Company B stopped by to see how Pa and the rest of their wounded were doing. Captain Carter, the Company Commander, introduced himself and then he asked me about Pa.

"He's doing as well as can be expected," I told him. "The doctor says he's lucky to be alive. We just need to wait and watch. He was very lucky that the minie ball didn't smash any bones."

He told me that several units had suffered many more casualties than the 8th, which numbered six dead and twenty-six wounded. While the Captain was talking, I remembered the folded tatter of paper I'd been keeping in my pocket. It was the letter I promised to deliver to John Lanham's son, if

★ ★ ★

I finally found Company B. It was the least I could do to repay John's kindnesses to us. I hoped that I wasn't too late. What if John's son was one of those who died on the battlefield?

"Sir, do you know a soldier named Lanham? I promised his pa that I'd give this here letter to him. I almost forgot all about it."

But before the Captain had time to reply, a soldier standing behind him said, "I'm Lanham. Sam Lanham," and a handsome young lad of about eighteen stepped into view.

I looked at the folded scrap of paper and held it out to him. "If your pa is John Lanham of Salem Station, then this is for you. He asked me to give you this if I found you. I'm afraid it's gotten a bit worn in my pocket." Sam stepped forward and took the letter from me. He held the letter tentatively in his hand as I continued. "Your pa said it was important for you to get it. He said you two had harsh words before you left. He hoped this would mend some of the hurt."

Sam looked down at the letter, all the while running his fingers back and forth over the folded paper. Then he tucked it hastily into his shirt pocket and muttered, "Yeah, I'm John's son. Now you done your part and I thank you for that. But I'm not sure I'm ready to read this just yet," and he wheeled around and left the tent.

I looked at the Captain and asked, "Did I do something wrong? He didn't seem very happy. I was thinkin' he'd like to get a letter from his pa."

But the Captain looked out at the retreating form of the young soldier and said, "No, son. You did the right thing. It's just something between Sam and his father. You see, like

★ ★ ★

a lot of young men, his father didn't want him to enlist, but Sam went anyway. They parted company with hard words and it's been eating away at young Lanham ever since, even though he was determined to join the 8th and be part of fighting for the South. But Sam'll have to come to terms with his father and his decision sooner or later. That letter is just making him face old problems again. You did what you said you would do and now Sam just has to work it through. Don't you worry yourself about him. You just take care of your father. As soon as he gets strong enough, you take him on back home. He'll be able to get his strength back much better there. The 8th's got to move on again, but we'll be thinking about you as we go."

The Captain left, and that's when I met Colonel Eppa Hunton, the Commander of the 8th Virginia. When he came in to see Pa, he said, "I wanted to meet the young man who went so bravely to his father's side in the midst of a dangerous battle. It's that kind of bravery that makes a fine soldier. I know he's very proud of you, too," and he reached out to shake my hand. Then he said, "As soon as your father is well enough to travel, you take him back home. Take good care of him and get him well. He's a good soldier and I know he's a good father. Maybe someday we'll all meet again under more peaceful circumstances." Neither of us knew then that we would, indeed, meet again, but unfortunately the circumstances would not be peaceful.

Those first few days, Pa was in and out of consciousness, waking every so often and looking at me, but not really seeing me. I felt so helpless. There was nothing much that I could do except just be there. I dreaded the moment when he would

★ ★ ★

wake up though, because then I would have to tell him all of our bad news.

Jessie came by occasionally with Jim Robinson, but we had early on decided that a battlefield hospital was no place for an eight-year-old girl to be, so she spent most of her time at Jim's house with his family. Eventually, Jim convinced me that I needed to get a full meal and a good night's sleep. He took my place by Pa.

When I returned early the next morning, Pa was awake. He smiled when he saw me. Me, I just started to cry. I couldn't help myself.

Kneeling beside his cot, I bawled, "Pa, oh, Pa. Jessie and me, we looked everywhere for you, Pa. But I let you down. I didn't do what you wanted me to do, and now it's too late. Pa, it's…it's…about Ma. Ma's…"

But before I could finish, Pa put his hand on my arm and said reassuringly, "It's all right, Jacob. I know about Ma. Jim here was sittin' with me late last night when I first woke up. He told me that you and Jessie were here and most of what happened. He knew I should know, and he knew that it was gonna be hard for you to tell me. But what happened to Ma wasn't your fault, son. You done everythin' that you could. I never should've left the three of you alone. You needed me and I wasn't there. If anyone is to blame, it's me."

"But, Pa. Squealer's gone, too. The bears got him and we…"

"Jacob, you done everythin' you could. I'm so proud of you. It takes a man to do everythin' you did. It took a lot of courage for you and Jessie to come and find me. This was so hard for the two of you. But I promise as soon as I'm strong

★ ★ ★

enough, we're gonna go back home. Back home together! It won't be the same, I know, but we'll try our best. And I won't never leave you two again."

8
Going Back Home, September, 1861

Dramus had carried Pa off to war, and now the mule was bringing us all back home. James Robinson had loaned us a small cart, which we promised to return whenever we could.

We rumbled slowly down the Alexandria-Warrenton Turnpike headed west. Jessie curled up on a pile of straw with the goat and her cat. She had been so excited about taking Pa home, that after a few miles of jostling along, she fell asleep. I watched Pa as he urged Dramus down the dusty turnpike. I'd been trying for days to find a time to talk to Pa alone. There were so many things happening around me and I just couldn't sort them out by myself. For awhile Pa had been too tired and too weak to talk. But now I couldn't wait any longer and this seemed like the perfect time.

"Pa, why are we fightin' this war? Why are the Federals fightin' this war? I just don't understand what is so important that men are willin' to kill each other over it. I just don't understand."

As I waited for him to answer, I noticed how very tired and old he looked, much older than his thirty-two years. I decided that war and killing could probably do that to a person.

When Pa spoke, it was in a very low, soft voice and I had to lean closer to him to hear. "Son, I thought I knew why I

★ ★ ★

was fightin' this war. I also thought there wouldn't even be much of a fight when the Feds saw that we meant to stand up for our rights. But after this stand at Manassas, I think we are just seein' the beginnin' of this war. It ain't gonna be quick and it ain't gonna be easy. I went into this here war because everyone was sayin' that the South was gonna have our own Confederation of States, just like the United States, but we was gonna make sure the laws and rules were best for us Southerners. George Washington fought for the first rights of Americans and led a rebellion against injustice, and that's just what we meant to do. We know what's best for Virginians, and the Congress just wasn't payin' no attention. As for me, I was wishin' they could've found a better way to make their point. But like I said before to you, a man's gotta do what a man's gotta do. Some of the young men in our units just couldn't wait for the fightin' to begin. They hated the drillin' and marchin'. They wanted some action. But I know the battle the other day changed their minds. They saw more blood and dyin' than most men see in a lifetime. You saw it, too. Between the smoke and roar of the guns and cannons, it was impossible to even know who you were shooting at. A goodly number of men from both sides realized they didn't have the stomach for such fightin' and killin' and so they deserted. They ran off into the woods, both Union and Confederate. They're out there somewhere lookin' for places to hide.

"As for the Feds, why are they fightin', you ask? To preserve the Union they sez. What difference does it make to them? They come down here to our homes and farms, where our wives and families live, and they expect us to just let

★ ★ ★

them move right in and take over. Well, no man is gonna push me around and take over the land and family that means so much to me. No one's gonna tell me how to run my farm. No Yankee is gonna take my land. Mr. President Lincoln, he's got himself in a mighty big fix. He's callin' us the aggressors. All we're doin' is standin' our ground where we live. All those troops he's mustered from up North are marchin' down here into our precious Virginia and they still can't beat us. The fellas at the hospital camp said those Yankee boys couldn't run fast enough to get across the stone bridge to go back to Washington. They said some of them fine ladies and gents from Washington who thought they'd have a picnic and watch the fightin' had the fightin' come to them. Why, many of those fancy folks got caught up in the middle of those retreating cowards. Those Feds was runnin' right over top of them and all their finery as they panicked and ran away.

"We Virginians been takin' care of ourselves since this state began. George Washington, Thomas Jefferson, and many other fine Virginians set up this state, and we don't need any President or Congress makin' unfair decisions about how our state should run. We Virginians know what's best for Virginia. So that's what I'm fightin' for. I don't expect you can fully understand, but you've seen more than most young'uns. The sights at the battlefield certainly made even those who believed strongest in the cause question why, just as you have. But we cannot allow those who died to die in vain. We must be united in our efforts to govern ourselves as we see fit. And in doing so, God help us all."

With those words and in that moment I saw in Pa's eyes

★ ★ ★

a determination I had never seen before. I could feel the passion in his voice, and I began to sense some of the driving force which compelled men to stand up and fight. I had a sense of what Pa was fighting for, but I still didn't understand why the Yankees would come so far from their own homes to fight a battle that didn't seem to concern them. They weren't on their own land. They were being killed too. For what? Pa had given me some answers, but I still had more questions. I wondered if anyone really understood how wars began. What problems could be so bad that killing other men could be the only solution? It was something I would have to think about. What could justify that grim scene that was etched so firmly in my mind?

"Pa, I just can't stop thinkin' about all those men dyin' on the field around us that day. Didn't matter if they was Yanks or Rebs 'cause they didn't look no different. Their blood was red and they all cried out the same. You think there's gonna be more fights like that?"

"Son, I think this is just the beginnin'. I hope I'm wrong, but there are lots of other folks that seem to feel the same as me. What you and I saw will be just a drop in the bucket before all this is over. We Confederates showed 'em at Manassas that we aren't foolin' around none. We mean to stand up and fight to the bitter end. We got 'em on the run and we'll keep it goin' that way."

"How long do you reckon all this will last?"

"Only God can answer that question, son, but I pray it won't be too long. Mostly I worry about you and your sister. I don't want anythin' to happen to either of you. With the fightin' this close to home, that ain't very comfortin'. Let's

★ ★ ★

hope that any further fightin' goes closer to Washington."

"Pa, would you go off to fight again, if'n you was able?"

"I'd do it again in a heartbeat if I was able. So many men and boys died out there on that field for both sides. My not fightin' ain't gonna stop the war. It'll only stop when somebody wins. I don't intend to let that be the Yankees. The sooner one side is the victor, the sooner we'll be able to settle back to what most of us knows best, and that's farmin'."

I sure hoped that all the fighting would be over before Pa ever felt well enough to fight again. I couldn't bear the thought that he might go off into another battle like the one we just were part of. This time he was only wounded. Next time he might not be so lucky.

As we bounced along, I could see the pain in Pa's face. "Pa, I can drive if you need me to, if it hurts your arm too much."

But Pa didn't respond and seemed to be deep in thought. I wondered what was going through his mind. Was Pa thinking about what lay ahead for us? Was he thinking about Ma, his Annie? I couldn't imagine returning home and not having her there to greet us. It surely had to be difficult for him. She had always been right there beside him. Farm life was not easy, but Ma never complained. Now I wondered if he worried about whether he would be able to take care of the farm and us by himself. Pa was still weak and we didn't know if he would ever be able to fully use his left arm again. I was strong, though, and I'd just turned twelve, but I knew I couldn't handle all the work on the farm by myself. Ma had always done so much, too. Who would take over all the jobs

★ ★ ★

that she had done? Jessie, at eight, was still too young to take over the womanly chores. She had been learning to help Ma, but she still had so much more to learn before she could run the house on her own. Who would tend the vegetable garden and prepare the meals and do the laundry and make the soap and mend the clothes and…. As the list in my mind grew longer and longer, I wondered if the same thoughts were going through Pa's head as he stared off in the distance.

Eventually, Pa looked down at me, as if finally remembering my question, and replied, "That's all right, son. I'll let you know if I'm uncomfortable. I know I can always count on you if I need anything."

I cringed at those words. That's what Pa had said as he went off to fight in the war, and look at what had happened. Ma had died and Squealer was gone. How could I be counted on for anything?

Pa must have seen the troubled look on my face. My expression often gave me away, especially when I felt I was not living up to Pa's expectations.

"Son, you've been through some mighty tough times. You had to take care of situations that woulda made a grown man weak in the knees. Your decisions were good ones. Don't second guess yourself. I know you keep thinkin', 'What if I did this?' an' 'What if I done that?'. It don't matter now. What you done was the best you could do. I know you worry about Ma. It's a terrible thing that happened, but it wasn't your fault. There wasn't nothin' you coulda done different or better'n you did. You can't spend the rest of your life blamin' yourself. I miss your Ma, too, but it eases my mind some to know that you an' Jessie was there at the end takin' care of

★ ★ ★

her. I know that she's up there somewhere right now smilin' down at us and watchin' us go home. And she'll always be there watchin' over us. So you just get those dark clouds outta your head. We'll miss her dearly, but we're gonna be all right. You got that, boy?"

I really needed to hear those words from Pa. I did feel responsible for all that had happened. Pa saying I had done the right things helped to heal the blame I'd been keeping locked inside. I'd always wondered if there wasn't something else I could have done. But it felt good to have Pa beside me again. He leaned over and put his good arm around my shoulder as we continued down the road. If the mule held out and there was no rain, we could be home by nightfall.

9
Strangers in the House

As we turned down the lane to the cabin, the last rays of sun were fading behind pink mottled clouds. Jessie was awake now and the three of us sat side by side on the seat. The tall tasseled corn stood like rows of silent sentinels as we passed by. The sight of that corn was a welcome sign, as there would be food for the animals and some to grind for bread and porridge. It was almost dark as we neared the house, and we were not ready for the dismal scene we saw. Tangled weeds had taken over in the yard and the garden. It was no longer the neat place Ma had always taken care of. The front door was open a bit. I had a strange sensation that something wasn't right. Pa pulled up the mule and I jumped down from the wagon.

★ ★ ★

"Wait here, Jess, and hold onto Dramus' reins while we get a light in the house," Pa cautioned. "We'll be right back." Pa's injuries forced him to move a little slower, but he wasn't too far behind me.

I was first to get to the door. I was sure I had closed it tight before we left. I felt the hairs on the back of my neck stand on end. I thought about the deserters that Pa told me about earlier. I hesitated momentarily, then stepped cautiously into the inky blackness. I felt my way toward the table, my hands reaching into space. My hip bumped into the table and I continued to feel my way slowly along its edge until I thought I was where the lantern should be. Then I reached forward in the darkness. Something warm moved under my hand and a loud, piercing shriek filled the air. Someone grabbed my arm from one side, gouging me with sharp nails. Someone else screeched at me from the other side. I screamed out in pain and covered my face from the repeated blows of the attackers. I fell to the floor with my arms over my head. I couldn't tell how many there were. They just kept banging away at me from all sides. It seemed forever before Pa came running in. The shrieking was loud and came from every direction. Grabbing the first thing he saw, Pa began to flail at the screaming, clawing attackers with Ma's broom. Running left and right and every which way to get away from Pa's blows, the enraged intruders flapped and scrambled out into the yard. I lay on the floor, my head and face covered by my arms and my heart pounding. It took several minutes before I realized that I hadn't been attacked by deserting soldiers, but rather by a bunch of deserted chickens. The flock that Jessie and I had left behind to fend for themselves had taken to roosting

★ ★ ★

in the house and were not the least bit happy when I disturbed them once they had settled down for the night.

Pa helped me to my feet, my heart still pounding like a drum. "That was a close one," I gasped. "I was sure we'd been invaded by some Yankee deserters."

"Just stand still, Jacob, and I'll try to find us a light. Then we'll see what damage those chickens did to you and to the house." Eventually, a small light flickered at the far side of the room as Pa found the lucifers near the fireplace and lit the lantern hanging beside it.

Outside Jessie was yelling, "Pa! Jacob! Are you all right? What's all that noise?"

"Everything's fine, little girl," Pa yelled back. "You can come in now." After checking me over, we decided I was more scared than hurt by the trespassing chickens. Pa sent me out to unhitch Dramus and take care of the animals. I returned shortly with a bucket of fresh, warm milk from Nanny. At least we would have something to drink that night.

★ ★ ★

10
Much Work to be Done

We very quickly realized what a huge amount of work lay ahead of us. Often I would catch Pa grimacing with pain, as he attempted to do some of the more strenuous tasks. Most of the time, his pain was caused by the bullet wound, which was still healing, but sometimes I think it was because he missed Ma. It had to be hard to face that she was gone from him forever. He never cried. Pa wouldn't cry. But the smile he had always worn was now replaced with a frown, which settled deep into his brow.

Pa gave the orders and we all worked to try to get the house and grounds back into some sense of order. I worked outside, caring for the animals and checking out the fields and grounds. Pa helped Jessie in the house as much as he could. He quickly realized that he was not able to do his share of the work yet. He tired easily and certain movements caused him a lot of pain. He tried not to let us see, but we had already realized that Pa was not the same man who had ridden away from us last May. The smile was gone and his strength was lessened. Jessie and I knew that we were going to have to rely on each other just as we had when we had journeyed to find him. We thought that finding Pa would solve all our problems. But now that we were home, we wondered if we would ever really have Pa back. Our Pa with the smiling face and laughing eyes. The Pa who delighted in picking us up and tossing us in the air. The Pa who we could count on for anything, anytime. Ma was gone, and now we sensed that the Pa we knew before the war was gone, too. Would he ever return?

★ ★ ★

The next couple of weeks were very busy ones. With all our efforts, the farm was looking almost like it had before we left. The main crops of corn and wheat were not all lost and would provide food and feed. There was, however, no time for play or fun. Pa's temper was much shorter now. Before all this he had been fun to be with, laughing and joking. But now he seemed to scold us at the slightest provocation.

The journey to find Pa had increased that special bond that existed between Jessie and me. Our adventures, both good and bad, continued to be a source of conversation whenever we had time together. Jessie and I laughed remembering how Squealer had dragged her through the dirt and mud trying to get to a stream to drink. He had been a lot of fun, even though he had caused us so many problems. Now his empty pigpen was a source of more hard feelings with Pa. He had told us time and again not to name our pigs since they were intended to be food, not pets. But Squealer had been different. Since we had returned, Pa had remarked more than once that food would be tight for us come winter without the hams and salted meats that a pig would have supplied. But Jessie and I would not have let Squealer become ham and bacon without a good bit of protest. However, an angry mother bear had eliminated that concern, and all because Squealer had been too piggish to share some peaches. Jessie and I did miss that fat little troublemaker.

Though we might be short on meat, Jessie had managed to salvage some things in Ma's kitchen garden. Once she had pulled the overgrown weeds, she revealed surviving squashes, beans, and herbs. Our root crops of potatoes, onions, yams, turnips and beets had been safely protected beneath the earth.

★ ★ ★

We dug them up and stored them in the cool root cellar. Our apple trees in the back field had an abundant harvest that year. We didn't go hungry that winter, but we didn't have the variety of foods that Ma would have prepared for us. She knew just what to do and when to do it. All her recipes were in her head, and she had learned them from her mother when she was little. Jessie and I had watched Ma and learned some of her special dishes, and Pa had even learned a few, but we knew that most of her best recipes were gone with her forever.

11
An Unexpected Visitor

One day that fall when I was plowing the far field with Dramus in preparation for the winter wheat, I looked up and saw a wagon coming down our lane. People rarely came out our way. I watched as Pa walked out to meet the wagon, and then saw Jessie run up to greet the driver. I unhitched Dramus from the plow and rode him back to the house. By the time I got there, everyone had gone into the house.

"Well, it's about time you showed up!" greeted me as I walked through the door. Standing there with his pipe in his mouth and a broad smile on his face was John Lanham. I was so surprised. "The cat got your tongue, boy?" he chuckled. "I at least expected a hello."

All I managed to stammer was, "Yessir. Uh, no sir. I mean, hello, sir. I see you already met my pa. And Pa, this is John Lanham, one of the men I told you about who was so helpful to us when we were lookin' for you. And you can see, we finally found our pa."

★ ★ ★

"That you did, my boy. That you did. And you also delivered my letter to my son. For that I am most grateful. Sam came to Salem Station a few days after the battle at Manassas. Sam was able to come home for a few days when the 8th was at nearby Waterford to guard the Potomac Crossin's. We had some long talks. He told me all about you findin' your pa, and how your pa had been hurt, and how you had saved his life. I wasn't surprised none, 'cause I knew you were a brave boy the minute I met you."

Before John could continue, Pa surprised Jessie and me by saying, "John, we'd be pleased if you'd join us for dinner and spend the night. That way we can catch up on all the news you have to share. I want to hear all about what is happenin' with my old company. I know the children would like for you to stay, too."

John agreed and then added, "I even brought you all some of my special peach preserves and some honey."

John's mention of peaches reminded me, "I don't guess you heard about what happened to our pig, Squealer, after we left your place."

"As a matter of fact, I did. And that brings me to the most important reason for my comin' here. I think that you and your sister need to come out to the wagon with me to bring in some of my goodies before we go any further." I saw John give Pa a wink as we went out the door together. Pa stood there watching with a puzzled look on his face.

John told me, "Jacob, go uncover that big crate under the straw in the back of the wagon and see if you can bring it down here." He gave Jessie a little nudge, too, saying, "You'd best go help him. I don't know if he can do this alone."

★ ★ ★

By the time Jessie got to the back of the wagon, I had climbed into the wagon bed and was pulling the straw off the large crate in the back. Both of us let out squeals of joy, which were echoed by several deep squeals from the crate. There, sitting big as life, was Squealer.

We opened the top of the crate and began to rub Squealer's head and ears. He was much bigger than when we had last seen him, and as we stroked his back, we saw several long, thick ugly rows of scars. We didn't need anyone to tell us what had caused them. Squealer snorted contentedly as we rubbed and nuzzled his scarred old body.

★ ★ ★

John walked with his usual limp to the back of the wagon. "I thought you would remember this ole guy. A day or so after you left, he showed up at my back door lookin' mighty poorly. Of course, I could tell from the claw marks what had gotten to him. I was mighty concerned that the bear might have gotten you two as well. The worst part was I had no way of knowin' what direction Squealer had come from and so I didn't know where to begin to look for you. For the next few days, when I wasn't puttin' salve on the pig and tendin' to his wounds, I was sittin' on the porch watchin' and hopin' for you two to show up. I was worried sick about both of you. That's the state I was in when my Sam finally came home, told me you were both safe, that you had found your father, and that you had delivered my letter. But now, let's get this big guy out of here and back into his own pen where he belongs."

Pa came out to the wagon and listened to all the commotion. I couldn't help but notice the furrow in his brow deepen as he watched all of us together. This was why he never wanted us to make pets of animals that were going to have to be slaughtered. This was going to present a difficult situation that I knew he wished he would not have to deal with. We could really use some ham and bacon and lard to get through the winter. I understood that. But somehow I thought this might be different.

Pa decided to let us enjoy that moment. He knew that situation would have to be faced another day. I suspected he secretly wished John had never found that pig or nursed it back to health. We had already accepted its loss. Now it would have to be dealt with all over again. He did not want to have

★ ★ ★

to be the bearer of such news, but he knew it was going to have to come eventually. While we trotted gleefully out to the shed with Squealer, Pa on the other hand, trudged back to the house with an obviously heavy heart.

At the dinner table, John's smile and warm personality kept that evening cheerful. I think I was the only one who noticed the change in Pa's mood. Pa had been more serious since his return, but now, even with company, his mood had not improved at all. If anything it had gotten worse. At least, I thought, with John here, tonight would be fun.

We took turns telling John everything that had happened to us after we left his house, beginning with the encounter with the bears and ending with finding Pa and bringing him home. John listened to us thoughtfully. When we finished, he said, "Seems everyone was proud of you, and I was proud, too, when I heard some of that story from my Sam." John looked at Pa and said, "I know you must be proud of your children, too."

Pa nodded, saying, "He and Jessie are very special to me. I don't know what I would do without them. Jacob's as fine a son as any man could ever hope for and Jessie brightens our days. I'm a very lucky man. But now if it's all right with you two, I want to hear John's news about what's been goin' on with the 8th Virginia since they left Manassas. The last I heard, they was headed up to the Potomac."

Jessie and I cleaned up and then went to bed. We fell asleep that night to the droning sound of the men's voices.

The next morning we waved goodbye as John drove off, having promised to visit us again when things settled down. Then Jessie and I ran off to the shed to feed Squealer and

★ ★ ★

give him a good rub down. Pa followed us to the shed, the furrow deepening in his brow. I saw him watching us, and I knew from the determined look on his face what he must be thinking. A pig has a purpose on this farm, and that purpose is to supply us with meat for the winter. As Pa turned away to go back to the house, I saw him kick the ground angrily. I knew that look on Pa's face. It was only a matter of time before Squealer was headed for the butcher's block. And sooner or later it was Pa who would have to break that news. I watched Jessie laughing and petting Squealer, and I thought to myself, why did you have to come back anyhow? You're just going to cause us a lot more trouble and unhappiness.

12
Jessie's Visit to Town

That year October was mild and our trees were ablaze of golden autumn colors. Things were going along as well as we could hope for. The crops and the fields were cared for, and Pa's wound seemed to be mending gradually, but well. He decided it was time to go to Warrenton for a few supplies and to return Jim Robinson's wagon. Pa would find someone to drive the wagon down the turnpike and drop it off at Jim's. There had been no hurry to do this, and that was good, because with all the work that we'd had to do on the farm, there was little time for a trip to town. Anything Pa might bring back from town would just have to fit behind him on Dramus. A vee of geese honked high overhead as Pa headed off.

When he returned late that evening, Jessie and I were waiting for him. We could tell by the look on his face that

★ ★ ★

he'd gotten more war news. He began talking as soon as he dismounted.

"There's been another battle up at Ball's Bluff near Leesburg. The 8th was in the thick of it. Union troops started shootin' and comin' across the Potomac. We were outnumbered and they still couldn't beat us. Lots of casualties though. For sure the Feds are gonna think twice about takin' us on again." He continued as we walked to the house, "The Yankees are even blockadin' the turnpike and not lettin' goods get through to town. Many necessary items are gettin' scarce and the prices of those that are available are goin' sky high. And it's only gonna get worse. We're gonna have to be careful with what we've got stocked up out here."

Pa's trip into Warrenton had put a new sense of energy into him. We hadn't seen him this alive since before he went away to join the Army. The news of the success of the 8th Virginia at Ball's Bluff had gotten his dander up about the war again.

It wasn't too long after that when Pa said, "I need to go to Warrenton with our wagon to try to get a few more winter supplies if they're to be had. I'll be stayin' overnight this time. I thought maybe Jessie might like to come with me. There's a place in town that'll put us up. Jacob, you can go another time, but now someone's got to stay and look after the animals. Is that all right with you?"

I saw Jessie's face light up when she heard Pa's suggestion. I was disappointed I couldn't go, but Pa was right. Someone had to stay behind and Jessie couldn't do it. "I don't mind, Pa. Besides, Jessie would like that."

Jessie was so excited that she raced over and gave me a

★ ★ ★

big hug. "Oh, thank you, Jacob. I wouldn't go if you wanted me to stay, but I'd really love to go with Pa."

And so it was settled. The next morning they hitched up Dramus and headed down the road. Jessie kept waving back to me until she couldn't be seen anymore. It was later that Jessie would fill me in on the details of that trip. Certain events of that visit would have a greater effect on our lives than either of us ever realized at the time.

Jessie and Pa noticed as they rode into town that a lot of farm fields were not plowed and many people's fences had been torn down or were missing. Pa said that was not a good sign. Probably the result of troops moving around through the area.

In town Pa ordered what supplies he could get, and then they went on to Mrs. Chalmer's boarding house. Mrs. Chalmer's was a small, two-story building on the edge of town. Although things appeared bare and dreary on the outside, the people inside were warm and friendly.

"It's good to see you again, Nate," said a man rocking in a corner. "Got your girl with you this time, I see."

"Yup. This here's Jessie. And how are you doin', Tom?" Pa replied. "You weren't lookin' all that good the last time I was here."

"I'm as well as can be expected. The ladies here have nursed me through this sickness. Reckon I'll be headin' back to our unit real soon though."

"Glad to hear that. I'd like to be goin' with you, but that's just not possible yet." Pa put his hand to his shoulder as he spoke. "What's the latest from the troops?"

"The big news is still the fight at Ball's Bluff on October

★ ★ ★

21st. The 8th sure showed them a thing or two. A few of the local folks who went to tend to the dead and wounded said the scene at the top of the bluff was a horrible sight. Said the Union troops were so afraid that they tried to escape by jumping from the cliffs to get to the Potomac. The Union troops were in shambles. I'd have liked to have been there."

"We've got a unit to be proud of all right. They were victorious at Manassas and now again at Ball's Bluff. I wish I'd been there, too."

Jessie listened as the two men talked. She knew that Pa would have liked to have been able to stay with his unit and continue to fight. Instead, he was stuck on the farm taking care of two children and a bunch of animals. She could have been a part of the wall for all Pa knew, he was so caught up with all this news of the fighting. Only the entrance of a bustling middle-aged woman brought them all back into focus.

"Why, Nate Harding, I didn't hear you come in. Tom, you should have called me," she admonished. "Olivia, do see who has come by," she called into the other room, and then spotting Jessie, she asked, "And who is this sweet young lady with you?"

Before Pa could answer, a very pretty young woman quietly entered from the other room. She was dressed all in black and her dark hair was pulled back into a bun. She looked shy and a bit embarrassed when she saw Pa. "It's so nice to see you again, Mr. Harding," she said so softly that Jessie barely heard her. The woman kept her eyes lowered and looked at the floor as she spoke.

"It's nice to see you again, Mrs. Carter," Pa replied rather

★ ★ ★

nervously. Then he remembered Jessie and said, "This is my daughter, Jessie. She's come to town with me. Thought it would do her some good to see some women folk for a change. Jessie, this is Mrs. Chalmer and this is Mrs. Carter."

Mrs. Chalmer put her arm around Jessie and said, "Why don't you come into the kitchen with Olivia and me, and we'll leave these two men alone to catch up on things. You can tell us all about how you and your brother found your pa, and how things are going along out at your place." They made Jessie feel very at ease. She was so glad that Pa had asked her to come along. She was just sorry that this visit was not going to be longer. She hadn't realized how much she'd missed Ma and being able to talk to some ladies.

Time flew by at Mrs. Chalmer's house. Dinner was served for everyone who was staying at the house. Everyone talked on endlessly about the fighting and the lack of goods. Jessie listened and took it all in. She said she wanted to remember every detail to tell me.

13
Pa Comes to the Rescue

The next morning Pa got Jessie up early. They still had to pick up their supplies, and then they would have the long ride home. Pa drove down a side street in town and pulled the wagon up to a store. As he tied up the mule, he told Jessie, "Wait out here. I'll be right back."

Jessie nodded her head and sat back. She was reliving all the conversation and fun of the previous evening. She told me that she never heard the footsteps approaching the wagon,

★ ★ ★

she only remembered hearing a raspy voice behind her snarl, "Well, well. If it ain't that purty little lady with the goat. And where's your big, brave brother?"

Jessie recognized that horrible voice immediately. Her knees began to tremble and she felt as though she was going to faint. She was so frightened that she couldn't move. A rough, calloused hand grabbed her arm, and then the gnarly face of Vergil Turner pushed up close beside her. He was even uglier than she had remembered.

Purple faced with a scraggly beard, he sneered up at her as he pulled her down towards him. "Thought you'd seen the last of me, eh, little girl? Well, nobody gets the best of Vergil Turner, nobody. Where's that brother of yours? He's the one I really want. Him and that nasty goat of his. I told you two that I'd better not ever catch you again if you knew what was good for you."

Jessie held onto the wooden seat with one hand as Vergil yanked at her, trying to drag her off the wagon. She worked to wrench her arm free from this vile, smelly old man. She wanted to scream, but nothing came out, except a little squeak.

"Let go, you little brat," he growled as he gave her arm a hard yank.

Jessie's hand was losing the hold she had on the wagon, and she felt herself slipping into Vergil's grasp. Just then Pa came around the corner. He dropped the sack of flour he was carrying and grabbed the old man by his shirt front.

"Let go of her, old man, or you'll never see the light of another day," Pa yelled. Vergil released his grip on Jessie, and Pa threw him to the ground. "Don't you ever touch my daughter again or I'll make sure you never touch anythin'

★ ★ ★

LOOKING BACK

again." Pa's face was red with rage as he glared down at the old man. Pa picked Jessie up in his arms and hugged her tight. "Now get outta my sight before I really lose my temper," he bellowed at Vergil.

Cowering, Vergil crawled off a little ways before he dared get to his feet. Slowly, he hobbled away, muttering to himself and brushing off the dirt. But all the time he kept glancing back to make sure that Pa wasn't coming after him again.

"Are you all right, Jess? I never would have left you alone if I thought anythin' like this would happen."

"P-Pa, th-th-that was the old m-man who tried t-to lock Jacob and m-me up at his house," Jessie stammered through her tears. "He scares m-me so much. I'm so glad you w-were here this time."

"Me, too, Jess. Me, too. It's lucky for him that I didn't know he was responsible for causin' all your trouble before. I mightn't a been so kind when I let him crawl off. But I don't think he'll come a botherin' you anymore now that he knows I'm back home."

14
Slaughter Time Comes

A cold, gray November day brought the moment that we had dreaded. "It's gettin' late in the season and there's a chill in the air. Slaughter time has come. I can put it off no longer," Pa announced to us with finality in his voice.

Jessie looked pleadingly at me, and I stepped forward and said, "But, Pa..."

"There'll be no buts, young man." He raised his voice in a

★ ★ ★

threatening tone. "I told you and told you not to make pets of the livestock. It only brings pain. I waited as long as I could, but that's all there is to it. I can wait no longer. We need everythin' that animal supplies for us: the meat for food and the lard for soap and cooking. Tomorrow I'll take care of it. You don't have to be there. I'll do it by myself. Now, not another word."

I'd never heard this tone in Pa's voice and the look on his face said that this was no time to argue. It was downright frightening. Jessie, her hands over her face, rushed out the door crying. I stood there alone, afraid to move, afraid to talk. Pa turned and strode to the fireplace, then stood with his back to me, staring into the fire. I turned quietly and went outside.

I wanted to find Jessie to explain why I hadn't tried harder to save the pig. I finally found her in the pigpen, with her arms wrapped around Squealer's neck, sobbing into his big, fat, scarred side. Squealer, oblivious to his impending doom, stood munching on an old corncob.

"You silly old pig," I murmured. "Why do you always cause us so much trouble?"

Jessie looked at me. She was a pitiful sight, all red-eyed and smudged with dirt. "Jacob," she sobbed, "d-do y-you th-think we c-could hide Squ-Squealer s-somewhere? Th-then m-maybe P-Pa w-would f-forget about h-him?"

Lifting my sister and guiding her away, I explained, "You know that ain't possible. First of all, there's no place big enough to hide him, and, second of all, we couldn't do that to Pa. I don't agree with him, but he's our pa and we gotta do what he says. Come on with me now." But I couldn't help myself as I turned around and whispered back at the pig, "We're sure gonna miss you, ole boy."

★ ★ ★

That night we went to sleep to the clicking sounds of Pa sharpening his knives against the honing stone. He was getting ready for the grim task ahead of him the next day. Each click went through us like a sharp, cold arrow.

The next morning was dark and overcast, like the mood of the house. No one spoke. Pa ate quickly and then went outside to fill the huge pots with water and set them to boiling. Jessie started to cry again, and I knew that nothing I could say was going to make things better. The last time I had a day this grim was the day Mama died.

I sat in front of the house mindlessly whittling a piece of wood. I needed to keep busy. I looked up and saw a cloud of dust in the distance. Someone was coming down the road. Who could it be? Finally I could make out the familiar face of John Lanham on a mule. I ran and shouted to Jessie, "It's John! John Lanham's coming. Hurry." Then I took off running down the road towards the approaching mule. Boy, did we ever need to see a happy face today. John couldn't have picked a better time to come.

John swung himself down from the mule. "My goodness. Why the long faces? Your pa hasn't taken a turn for the worse, has he? You two look terrible."

Jessie began to cry again, and I told him about Squealer's impending doom. "I'm mighty sad to hear that," John murmured, "but I can't say I didn't know. That's why I've come. What your pa's doin' is a tough job for a man to do alone, and he knew he couldn't ask you to help. He knew that you young un's were not goin' to take kindly to this. He asked me to come and help him if I could. I hoped I'd arrive in time to give him a hand. I know that's not the kind of help you

★ ★ ★

wanted from me. But with all that is going on right now, these are very difficult times for all of us. And from what I see and hear, it isn't goin' to get better for a long while. We need to do what we can to prepare ourselves to get through some very tough times ahead. I know this is hard for you to understand, but you will understand as time goes on. War, and this *is* war, is not pleasant and not easy. It is a vile and hateful thing that destroys everythin' we care for. Let's hope we can all survive and prevail." He went with us to the house, then asked, "Where's your pa now?"

I nodded toward the shed. John turned and quietly headed in that direction.

Jessie whimpered to me, "Even our best friend isn't helping us. Everythin' is happenin' because of this dumb ole war. I hate it. I hate everythin' it's doin' to us." Then she grit her teeth, and cried out loudly, "I hate it! I hate it! I hate it!"

15
The Burlap Sacks

When Pa and John came in for dinner late that night, they had cleaned themselves up carefully. I knew that this was a messy and difficult job. Ma and I had always helped before. I felt guilty that I hadn't even offered to help, but I knew I couldn't have done anything to hurt Squealer. Pa and John each carried in a burlap sack and put them on the floor. Then they sat down at the table.

Jessie and I had set the table and waited for the men. While we were waiting, we had promised each other we would

★ ★ ★

never ever eat another mouthful of ham or bacon as long as we lived. At dinner no one spoke. Each bite I ate had no taste and went down my throat in a lump. Then I heard a little squeal. I glanced at Jessie. She heard it, too. It was coming from the burlap bags. The burlap was moving on the floor.

Pa and John looked at each other, and then Pa said to Jessie and me, "I think you two better go check what's over there, right quick."

"And be a tad gentle while you're at it," John added.

As we each opened a squirming bag, the squealing got louder. Inside each one was a small pink piglet.

"I know this can't make up for Squealer," Pa said, "but it's the best I could do. These are going to be tough times and we got to provide for ourselves. John worked mighty hard to find these little critters for you. Take care of them, but remember why we got them. If times were different, and I'd a had any other choice with Squealer, you know I woulda taken it. But we don't got much, and this war's not helpin' any. A man's gotta do what a man's gotta do."

★ ★ ★

I'd heard those words before when Pa went off to fight. It was probably not the last time I'd hear them.

"Thanks, Pa," I said. "I understand what you had to do, but I gotta admit, it's awful hard sometimes. I'm sorry I wasn't more help to you today. I know how much you needed me, but..."

Pa interrupted, "That's all right, son. You already had to make some mighty tough decisions. I figured I could manage this one alone if'n I had to. The night John brought back Squealer, we discussed how hard givin' him up would be for you two. Between us, we decided he should try to find someone willin' to sell a couple of piglets. I couldn't say anythin' in case he couldn't find any. It would have been worse to promise somethin' and not deliver. John had to do a lot of dealin' to get these two. Folks are holdin' on to everythin' they got right now. I'm mighty beholden to him for all his trouble."

"Now, Nate, you know I didn't mind one bit. I'm just glad I got here in time. I'd a been here sooner, but I had to wait 'til these little ones could be taken from the big old sow. Fortunately, this farmer owed me a favor." Then John warned with a frown, "There are more and more troops movin' through Northern Virginia, both Union and Confederate, and they're all hungry. It don't matter whether they're for us or agin' us, the results'll be the same. They'll be lookin' to take anythin' they can eat. And we'll be lucky if that's all they take." There was a tone of despair in John's voice that we hadn't heard before. John stayed on a few more days helping Pa. When he left, Pa filled John's burlap bags with a share of the meat, lard, and scrapple that they'd prepared.

★ ★ ★

Although Jessie and I enjoyed the antics of our newest arrivals, and were grateful for Pa's and John's thoughtfulness, we knew there would never be another Squealer in our lives. We would never again let a piglet find a place in our hearts, only to have them broken on some cold, gray day.

16
A Wet, Cold Winter

The frosts were heavy now, and our chores turned to indoor ones. Pa rode into town more frequently, always returning by nightfall. Jessie had no desire to go with him again after her encounter with Vergil. Pa wanted to keep up with all the war news. Things in town were getting worse he said. People were trying to get on with their lives, but with a blockade on, goods from the North and from Washington were getting more expensive. Pa often said he was glad that we lived so far out and were used to providing for ourselves. The 8th Virginia was wintering in Centreville, and he'd heard that a lot of the soldiers were sick. As a result, many of the men looked for every opportunity to come home. More than once Pa had been able to meet up with members of Company B in town.

Christmas came and went, and it was a quiet, somber one for us, without Ma to share it. Pa had bought some little candy bags for each of us, but that was the extent of our celebration that year. It passed like any other day.

As Pa tried to keep up with the latest word on the war and also on the whereabouts of his old unit, I realized more and more that he was with his unit in spirit even if he couldn't be with them physically. The war was definitely the most

★ ★ ★

important item on his mind, even more important than the farm, and I began to wonder if it was more important to Pa than Jessie and me.

He returned from one trip to town all worked up. "The Confederate Congress has passed a law to encourage re-enlistments to fill the ranks," he announced. "Most men, me included, only signed up for twelve months. That's 'cause we thought this would all be over right quick. Congress says anyone who re-enlists will get thirty days furlough at home and an additional bounty of fifty dollars. 'Course, I didn't sign up till May, but if I didn't have the responsibility of the farm, that would be a mighty temptin' offer."

"But Pa, your arm and shoulder are still not as strong as they should be," I objected.

"I know that. It was just wishful thinkin'. I know I can't leave you young'uns alone again. Still, I feel like I should be doin' more to bring this war to an end. The Virginia Brigade, including my old unit, is now under the command of General George Pickett. They'll be leaving Centreville soon. As I said before, my not fightin' ain't gonna stop the war. It'll only stop when one side wins. I don't intend to let that be the Yankees. The sooner one side is the victor, the sooner we'll be able to settle back to what most of us know best and that's farmin'." That was when I knew it was only a matter of time before Pa found a way to get back into the thick of things.

It turned out to be a wet and cold winter. Everything had that grim, gray look. Pa continued to go to town whenever the weather permitted. Each time he would come back full of the latest news on the whereabouts of various troops. He'd even watched his own regiment march down the turnpike on

★ ★ ★

their way south. With each visit, Pa returned home in happier spirits. It was good to see him feeling better.

After one of his trips, he told us, "Lots of the folks in town are tryin' to decide whether to stay there or try to find a more peaceful place to live. Many have no place else to go. Some of the families that lost their menfolk in battle are hardest hit. I feel bad for them. I wish we could share some of what little we got with them."

"Maybe we could, Pa. That way we could be helpin', too." After all, we could afford to share a bit of our provisions from the smokehouse and root cellar. We could especially share the hams and bacon since me and Jessie don't have much of an appetite for them."

"I'm glad you feel that way, son," he replied, only half hearing what I said. "I was sure you would want to help, too. I'm already prepared to make the offer the next time I get into town," he stated as he walked away. I wondered what Pa meant by "make an offer." Who would he make an offer to? I was a little confused, but figured I would find out eventually.

Most of our chores at this point were inside. We only had to go outside to take care of the animals. Pa repaired any broken farm tools. Jessie attempted to mend our clothes. She would plop a torn shirt down in her lap and say, "I can't do this. I need help, Pa."

And Pa replied, "Just keep tryin', Jessie girl. We'll just have to see what we can do about gettin' someone to teach you all these things."

If Ma was here she'd know exactly what to do, I thought to myself, but I couldn't say that out loud. That would just make Jessie feel worse.

★ ★ ★

17
Special Supplies

In April, just before it was time to start spring planting, Pa said he needed to go into town for some special supplies. He took the wagon saying, "This'll probably take a day or two. Be on your guard though, 'cause there's been Yankees movin' through the area. Don't stray from the house. We live far enough away from the main roads that we can't really be seen, but you never know who might be scoutin' around." He seemed nervous and fussed over little things in the house that he usually didn't bother with. He took Ma's old shears and trimmed his hair and his beard, something he hadn't done since he'd come home from Manassas. He dug deep down in the old chest and pulled out a shirt that he used to wear on special occasions. I figured he must be meeting up with some of his old unit. But Pa didn't say, and we didn't ask.

That night drenching spring rains began to pound on the roof with a steady rat-a-tat-tat. The wet weather forced us to stay inside. One day passed, then two, then three. Jessie ran to the door every time she thought she heard a wagon or clopping hooves.

"Jacob, you don't think anythin' has happened to Pa, do you?" she asked impatiently.

"He said he would be gone a couple of days. It's only been three. I'm sure you don't have to worry. Pa can take care of himself. It's just that we're not used to bein' alone again and it seems longer than it's been. I'm sure he'll be home soon. He's probably waitin' for the rain to let up some,"

★ ★ ★

I reassured her. I, too, could imagine all kinds of things happening to Pa. After all, if the Yanks were to spot a man riding alone, there's no telling what they might do. These were getting to be mighty troubling times.

At last, late on the evening of the fourth day, we heard a wagon grinding down the road. It was too dark to see clearly, but we could hear wheels splashing through puddles. I grabbed the lantern and stood at the door waiting for Pa to pull up. In the distance, I could make out a dark shape on the seat. As the wagon came closer, I realized there was someone with Pa. Who could it be? I held the lantern higher. Finally, Pa pulled the wagon around by the door. The figure next to him was wrapped in an old blanket to keep off the dampness and the chill of the night air. I peered into the night trying to recognize who it might be. Pa jumped down and ran around to the other side of the wagon. As he reached up to the huddled form, the blanket fell back and I saw a young woman with a sleeping child cradled in her arms.

Pa gently lifted her and the child from the seat and set them on the ground. The child murmured and stretched out an arm. The woman looked down and held the child closer to her. Jessie came out, too, and in that murky darkness, we all looked questioningly from one to the other. Pa finally spoke up as he put his arm around the woman, ushering her toward the front door, saying softly, "Let's get in out of the night air. Jacob, come on in for now. You can unhitch Dramus in a few minutes, but first there's someone I want you to meet."

Inside, the only sounds were the crackle of the fire and the swish of the lady's dress. Jessie and I stood together watching as Pa brought a chair over beside the fire for the young

★ ★ ★

woman to sit on. The child snuggled into her arms, still sound asleep. She reached up and brushed his hair back. I could see now that it was a little boy. The lady was quite pretty, though there seemed to be a sadness about her. She had big, brown eyes like a frightened deer, and her dark hair was pulled back under her bonnet. She was dressed all in black. The child was blond with fair skin. I wondered if he would have his mother's deer-like eyes when he woke.

"Jessie, you remember Olivia and her little boy, don't you?" Pa said, breaking the silence. "Well, she is now Mrs. Olivia Harding. She has become my wife and will be your new mother."

The room at that moment was in absolute silence. I thought I surely must have misunderstood what Pa said. I looked at Jessie, but she had already run to the woman's side. They were talking to each other, but I couldn't hear anything. Pa finally pushed me toward her, saying, "This here's my oldest, and his name is Jacob. I see you and Jessie remember meeting awhile back at Mrs. Chalmer's. And the sleepy little fella there is her son, Garrett."

The woman reached out with her free hand and said softly, "It's so good to see you again, Jessie, and I'm so pleased to meet you, Jacob. I've heard so much about you." Her voice was as sweet and smooth as fresh clover honey.

Jessie held her outstretched hand and bubbled, "I'm so glad you're here. Are you going to live with us now?"

But I didn't wait for her answer; I stepped forward, muttered, "How d'you do," then quickly turned and mumbled to Pa, "I'd best go out and take care of Dramus and the wagon now."

★ ★ ★

"You do that, son," Pa nodded while he pulled up another chair for himself beside Olivia and the child.

As I walked out the door, I heard Jessie crooning, "Oh, isn't he sweet," obviously talking about the child. No one cared about me. No one cared how I felt about this intrusion into our lives. I stomped out to the mule. I couldn't believe that Pa had done this. How could he bring another woman into our house? She was not my mother. She might be Pa's new wife, but she would *never* be my mother. Ma was dead. I could never forget her. How could Pa do this to her? To us? It wasn't right. I jerked at the mule, pulling him toward the barn. I decided I would spend the night in the barn with Dramus. I didn't want to go back in the house with all of *them*. I dawdled, taking my time unhitching the mule and feeding him. I looked at the back of the wagon loaded with boxes and bags and crates. *Her* stuff. While I was stomping and stamping around the barn muttering to myself, Pa came in.

"We need to unload some of Olivia's things tonight. These crates especially." Pa either was unaware of my mood or he was ignoring it. "We need to uncrate these sheep. We'll put them in with the pigs until we can fix up a better place tomorrow. I'll carry in a few of the bags tonight and the rest we can get in the mornin'."

Not only is there a new wife and her son, but we've got all her stuff and her sheep to take care of, too. It was more than I could stand. I wanted to say something to Pa, like, "How could you?" or "Why?", but the words wouldn't come out. I buried my head against Dramus' side as Pa busied himself with the sheep.

"There was another big battle a few days ago," he said as

★ ★ ★

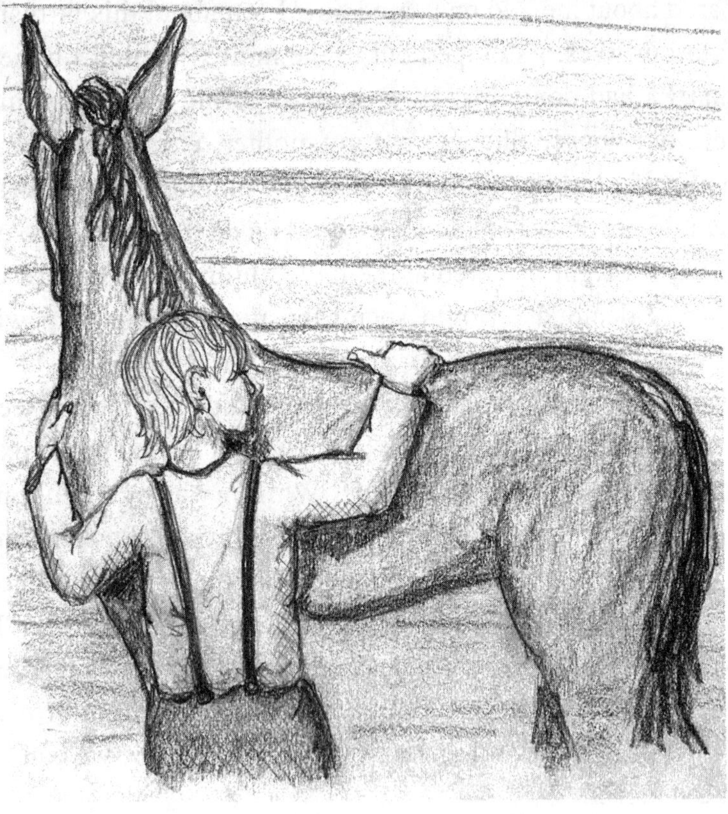

★ ★ ★

he worked. "A place called Shiloh in Tennessee. Folks said there were a lot of casualties. Reports keep comin' in, and when I left I still hadn't heard all of it. The Union seems to have gotten the best of that one. Every day brings news more alarmin' than the day before. I don't like all this killin'. I never thought it would come to this when everythin' started, but I'm afraid that there's no turnin' back now." Pa finished releasing the sheep into the pen, and then he came over to where I was still standing by the old mule.

"There's somethin' else I think you should know. It might help you understand. Olivia's husband was in the 8th Virginia with me," he explained. "He was wounded at Manassas, and they brought him to one of the hospitals that they set up in Warrenton. A cannonball hit right in front of him and he lost both legs. At first they thought they could save him, but he never pulled through. Olivia knew she couldn't care for their place by herself, and she had no family around. She decided to move into town, but with all the sick and wounded bein' cared for there, it wasn't a good place for her or for Garrett. Whenever I went into town I'd visit with her. As we talked, I explained that our family needed a woman here on the farm. Your ma did so much, and we just couldn't fill the emptiness that she left. I convinced Olivia that we both needed someone, that we needed each other. The final decidin' straw came a few days ago when Union troops occupied Warrenton. She didn't want to stay there. She was concerned about what people would think if she married again so soon, but she knew she had to take care of her son and herself. I just couldn't leave her and her child in circumstances like that. There was no tellin' how the Yanks would treat the townfolk. We decided

★ ★ ★

right then that this was the right thing to do. There was no time to talk to you or Jessie. That's what kept me so long. I don't know that you can fully understand now, but someday you will. I hope you'll help Olivia all you can. She's very kind, and she'll be especially good for your sister. And she'll be good for me, too," he concluded as he started toward the house. "Whenever you've got a mind to, come and join us in the house." And he left me alone to wrestle with my thoughts.

I was confused. News of Pa's marriage was shock enough, but now word that the Union forces were in control only a few miles away was also overwhelming. I wished I could just pull myself into a little ball and get away from everything. That wasn't going to happen and I knew I needed to face up to this situation.

I thought about Olivia. She did appear to be nice enough. Jessie seemed to like her. Would she expect me to call her Ma or Mother? I didn't think I could call her either. Calling her Mrs. Harding didn't seem right. Maybe I could just call her ma'am. That would be polite enough until I came up with something better. And then there was her son. Why couldn't he have been older? At least then he could have helped me with some of the chores. Now it seemed he'd be just one more job for me and Jessie.

The war always seemed far away from us. News such as this brought it closer and closer to home. I knew that if any Yank ever tried to come near this farm or this family, I would know exactly what to do without any hesitation. I could take on anyone who threatened us in any way. Then I began to realize what Pa had tried to explain to me when he first left to join the Army. A man's got to do what he thinks is right. And

★ ★ ★

now I was coming to that same sense of what I had to do. Home and family. That was what was important. Just like my Pa, I would do whatever was necessary to protect both.

I stood up and brushed the hay from my clothes, and I was ready to go back to the house. I found a new determination that would help me deal with any situation that this "present unpleasantness" brought our way. We would survive. That night, I walked back to the house a man. I'd left the boy I was behind.

18
Changes in Our House

Olivia's arrival brought many changes to our farm. She immediately assumed charge of the house, the kitchen, and the garden. That freed Pa and me to work full-time in the fields with the crops and the livestock. The best change came at meal times. Olivia took over the cooking that Pa, Jessie, and I had been doing as best we could. I tried to keep my distance from Olivia. But when I took my first bite of her beaten biscuits and her fluffy spoonbread, I just couldn't resist. And then when she put her first sweet potato pie on the table with those luscious, spicy smells wafting through the house, she really melted me down.

I watched Jessie blossom with Olivia's arrival. Now she had someone to show her how to do the things that she had just begun to learn from our own ma. She and Olivia laughed and chatted as they worked together. Garrett was a bundle of energy, but even at four, he was given his share of chores to do. Jessie took him with her wherever she went. Olivia was

★ ★ ★

able to work without worrying about him, and Jessie loved having someone to follow her and play with her all day long. At first I guess I was jealous. It used to be Jessie and me together. But now I was always in the field helping Pa, and Jessie had Olivia and Garrett to talk to all day. I reckon I had the most trouble adjusting. I felt left out. Even Pa seemed to forget about me and spent more time with them. Pa even started to smile some again, and I was the grumpy one.

Yet even though Pa's outlook improved with Olivia's arrival at the farm, Jessie and I knew that he was still not the happy, laughing Pa who had gone off to war a year ago. Sometimes I would catch him leaning on the fence and gazing off into the distance. I knew Pa still longed to be back fighting with the 8th, wherever they were. I was envious of Jessie and the way she and Olivia could talk. I wished that Pa and I could do that, too.

I stayed to myself a lot, doing my chores and feeling down on myself, and Pa kept up the best he could with the war. Towards the end of June, the 8th had some pretty tough fighting down in the Virginia peninsula, particularly at Gaines' Mill. I guess Pa might still have been thinking about fighting and I'd have still been feeling bad if it wasn't for our unexpected caller.

19
Cousins

It was near the end of July or the beginning of August. I know that because it was a terribly hot day before the second battle at Manassas. Pa and I were in the field wiping the sweat

★ ★ ★

off our faces, when we spotted this tall, dark-haired young fellow coming up the road. Now, we were being real careful of strangers, what with troops, both Union and Confederate, moving through the area and stealing any food they could get their hands on. While we were watching to see who it might be, I saw Olivia come out of the house and put her hand up to shade her eyes so she could see better. All of a sudden, she took off running down the dusty road toward him. The young man grabbed her up in his arms and swung her about in the air. Pa and I quickly went over to find out what was going on.

"Nate," she said, "I want you to meet my little brother, Conor. And Conor, this is my new husband, Nate Harding, and his son, Jacob." She was so happy and so excited. She held tight to his arm, her face beaming.

None of us had any idea at that moment the changes that Conor would bring to our lives, especially me.

That evening, Conor and Olivia told us how they were sent to live with different relatives after their parents died. Olivia stayed with an aunt and uncle in Virginia, and Conor went to live with a bachelor uncle who eventually moved to Maryland. When the war began, Maryland was wedged solidly between the Union and Confederate forces. President Lincoln decided to use any powers necessary to keep Maryland a part of the Union. He realized that Washington would be surrounded by Confederate states if Maryland decided to secede as Virginia had done. Conor's uncle was a Union sympathizer. He said his uncle became unbearable, and they argued a lot about the war. Conor wanted desperately to get back to Virginia, and to Olivia. His uncle said if he liked the

★ ★ ★

Confederacy so much, he could just pack up his belongings and go there. So that's what he did. He was determined first to find his sister. He learned that she had moved to Warrenton, and there he was told that she had married Nate Harding. He said the hardest part of his search was finding our place way out here. Pa explained that being way out here was what made this such a nice place. He invited Conor to stay on with us as long as he cared to. I was really glad because now there was someone near to my age to talk to, and also because that meant there was another strong back and pair of arms to help with all the heavy farm chores.

 Now to be proper about it, I should have called him Uncle Conor, after all, he was my stepmother's brother. But since we were so close in age, him being fifteen and me being almost thirteen, we decided to say we were cousins. He was what most folks would call a right handsome lad. His dark brown eyes always had a devilish twinkle combined with a bright, winning smile. The two of us hit it off right away.

 It didn't take me long to find out that life with Conor around would be anything but boring. He was not one to just sit around doing nothing. If something caught his eye, he'd be off to check it out. I could see why he might have had some problems getting along with his uncle. Conor was constantly thinking about new places to go and new things to do. He was always ready for adventure. With so much going on in his head, I could understand why he would have difficulty remembering the trivial chores he was supposed to do, like forgetting to latch the gate by the barn and letting the animals get out. Then everyone else would have to drop everything to help round them up. Or forgetting to stir the stewpot

★ ★ ★

when Olivia asked him to and nearly burning our dinner to a crisp. Then there were his devilish tricks, like hiding in the garden and scaring Jess and Garrett half to death. They would be afraid to go back there for days. But it was his unpredictability that also made being with him so exciting. However, his impulsive nature was also destined to get us into several serious predicaments.

20
Excitement at Catlett Station, August 22, 1862

Our first adventure almost got us both killed. It all started when Pa said he needed to go for some supplies. Times were as uncertain as ever, and it was dangerous everywhere. We never knew for sure if Warrenton or anyplace else was occupied by Union troops or our own. But that day Conor convinced Pa that the two of us should go for the supplies since a couple of young boys would be less apt to be troubled by soldiers than a grown man. Pa wasn't too keen on it, but against his better judgement, he finally agreed. He decided we should try to get the few things he needed at Catlett Station instead of going all the way into Warrenton. He thought things would be safer there, and it was a bit closer. Conor and I figured if we left that afternoon we could get back late that night or early the next morning.

It began to rain just as we were about to leave. It was August, and we needed the rain for the crops, but Olivia didn't want us to go until the storms cleared. Conor flashed her one of his big smiles and reassured her that it was just a little shower, and we'd be just fine. So off we headed full of ourselves to

★ ★ ★

be free of work and out and about in the countryside. We didn't take Dramus since between the two of us we could carry the supply sacks over our shoulders. We headed due south through fields and woods, planning to end up on the road into Catlett. Conor's "little shower" became a heavy downpour. We slogged through the mud, the slick red clay oozing up between our toes. We were drenched to the skin, but it felt good in the thick summer heat. Dark, ominous clouds made it seem like night by the time we were almost to the station. Then, just ahead of us through the rain and dusky light appeared row upon row of tents stretched all along the Orange and Alexandria tracks. Conor could hardly control himself and wanted to take a closer look. I wasn't so sure that was a smart thing to do. But when Conor decided he wanted to do something, he was like a mule that wouldn't be budged to do otherwise. So we crept closer and soon realized that this was a large detachment of Union troops.

"Let's see what they're up to," he whispered breathlessly. Again I wasn't sure we should, but he got onto me, saying, "You aren't scared, are ya?"

"Not if you ain't," I lied.

"Let's go then. We might never get this close to the war agin." Looking back, I have to laugh now to think that we actually believed that this might be the closest we would ever come to the war.

Anyway, there I was creeping along behind Conor, and him getting so close to some of the tents that I could hear the voices inside. I was so scared, all I could do was hang onto the back of Conor's pants trying to slow him down, and him swatting at me trying to make me let go. The rain had let up

★ ★ ★

some and we moved along, slowly working our way toward the station itself. Most of the Yankees were huddled around their fires trying to stay dry. We were almost to the station when we heard a roll of thunder rip through the sky. It was immediately followed by a deafening Rebel yell. The thunder in the sky became one with the thunder of a thousand galloping hooves as Jeb Stuart's cavalry came down upon unsuspecting Union forces like a swirling tornado. Conor and I darted for cover, ducking under the wooden steps of the station. My teeth chattered so loudly I was afraid someone would hear them and discover us. I bit down on the collar of my shirt to silence them. In spite of the rain, fires were being set to anything that would blaze. We watched through the cracks in the steps for what seemed like forever as horses thundered all around us and guns were fired in every direction. Then the skies opened up in another torrential downpour.

★ ★ ★

We heard one of the horsemen yell out, "Have they burned down the bridge at Cedar Run yet?"

"We're tryin', but this rain is giving us fits," came the reply. "But meanwhile we need to cut their telegraph line. That'll help slow up General Pope and his men. We need someone who can scramble up a wet pole."

Before I realized what he was doing, Conor ran out from under the steps and shouted up to the man on horseback, "I can do it for you, sir. I can get up a tree faster than any ol' squirrel."

"You're on, son. Let me give you a boost up," the officer replied. He dismounted, handed Conor a tool to cut the wire, and then locked his hands together for Conor's foot. With bullets zinging all around them, Conor climbed up on the man's shoulders and shimmied his way up to the top of the pole and clipped the lines. There were shouts of "hurrah" as the lines fell limply to the ground and Conor slid back down to the ground. There wasn't time for congratulations or pats on the back as Yankee gunfire rang out all around them. The officer jumped back on his horse and everyone quickly dispersed. Conor raced back to the steps where I was still hiding.

"Now that's what I call fun!" Conor said breathlessly, as he plopped back down beside me.

I stared at him wide-eyed, my mouth hanging open. I felt I must be dreaming all this. But no, there was Conor dripping wet next to me and the sound of gunfire all around us. Then the fighting died down as quickly as it had begun. It was the middle of the night. Conor and I stayed huddled under the steps, not yet ready to leave our hiding place. Eventually we dozed off.

★ ★ ★

As the pink light of dawn broke through the wispy clouds, we finally dared to inch our way out. The scene we saw around us was one of utter chaos. Tents, tables, and wagons were overturned. Trunks and boxes were smashed and goods strewn about. Some of the wagons that were set afire the night before still smoldered. If anyone was around, we didn't see them.

We cautiously edged away from the building and then high-tailed it for home, mighty glad to be getting out of there in one piece. Conor talked all the way, going over every detail of what we had seen and done. It sure scared me, but Conor never seemed to be frightened by anything.

Of course, when we got home without the supplies and told the tale of what had happened, Pa and Olivia were very upset. Olivia was upset because we had come so close to being killed. Pa, on the other hand, was upset that we'd come back without his supplies. "You can't send boys to do a man's job," he said. But I think he really was upset that he hadn't been in the middle of the fight instead of us.

Later we learned that Jeb Stuart's raid at Catlett Station was just a prelude to a much bigger battle, the Second Battle at Manassas. The skirmish Conor and I witnessed was supposed to stop General Pope's northward movement. But Stuart's men had been unable to burn down the railroad bridge because of water-logged trestle timbers and high, raging water in Cedar Run, and the mission failed. As a result, Union supplies and troops continued to move by rail and road toward Manassas. We could see their dust rising up for miles around in the hot August sky.

A little more than a week later, news of that Manassas battle came right to our front door. Pa, Conor, and I were out

★ ★ ★

stacking hay, when we saw a couple of men walking unsteadily down our road. Pa started toward them and then yelled back to us to hurry. When we got closer, we realized that the two were Confederate soldiers. They were dusty, dirty, and totally exhausted. We helped support them and brought them to the house. We got them water from the well and Olivia fixed them something to eat. After that they told us what had happened in Manassas.

"We thank you folks for your fine hospitality. We just want you to know that we ain't deserters. We plan to go back to our units, but after all we been through, we just couldn't be this close to home and not go there. We'll go back to our unit as soon as we check on our families," said the first.

"We were with General Longstreet and General Lee," the other man continued. "Ole Stonewall Jackson was there first and he got things under control. We sure whupped them good at the same place as last year. I guess them Yankees just don't learn too good. We lost a lot of our boys as well. Tom and me, we were part of the group left behind for the burial detail. We did what we could, but we just couldn't dig enough graves for all them poor souls. When we learned that Lee was marchin' us into Maryland, Tom and me said we didn't want to be no aggressors goin' up North. We've already taught them Yanks a thing or two. That's when we decided to take a little side trip home."

Pa was full of questions for the two men, asking for details about the battle and, in particular, any news about the 8th Virginia. The men talked with Pa for a bit, but it was obvious that they wanted to get on their way. Again they thanked us and headed down the road.

★ ★ ★

Their visit made Pa edgier than ever. This was a repeat of the battle that he had fought in. He wanted to know more about what was happening. The two deserters, for that is what they truly were, had not told him enough. He needed more. Pa was impossible to live with for the next couple of weeks. His thoughts seemed to be elsewhere.

21
Pa's Biggest Surprise

One morning I was out taking care of the livestock; I was still responsible for Nanny, our goat, as well as for Olivia's three sheep. I also took care of Dramus. The pigs that John Lanham gave us had long ago been slaughtered and never replaced. Jessie tended to the chickens and her cat. We kept all of them under a watchful eye so no wandering soldier could steal them away. I looked up as I turned the sheep and goat out to graze and saw Pa riding off on Dramus. Where was Pa going, I wondered? He hadn't said anything about leaving. I finished with the animals and walked back to the house. Olivia was at the table making a batch of beaten biscuits.

"I saw Pa riding off on Dramus. Where'd he go?" I asked.

Olivia looked up from her cooking. Her answers were short and curt. "Said he had some business to tend to. Said he'd be back by dark." Then she continued pounding the dough. Thwack! Thwack! Thwack! She didn't look up and she didn't offer any further explanation. I could tell something was bothering her, but I didn't press her anymore. I went out to the field to find Conor. But he had no idea where

★ ★ ★

Pa went either. That evening, we found out why Olivia was upset.

Pa arrived home on the mule loaded down with packages. We all ran out to find out where he had been. Olivia, however, stood back by the house, watching. Jessie and Garrett jumped up and down beside Pa, and he reached in his pockets and pulled out a little candy treat for each of them. Meanwhile, Conor and I helped unfasten the rest of the packages and carried them into the house.

Once inside he handed a small packet to Olivia. The aroma of coffee reached our nostrils long before she opened it all the way. It was something no one had had in a long time.

"It was hard to come by, and cost me dearly, but I knew it would be a special treat for you," he said as he gave it to her.

But the biggest surprise was yet to come as he spread a butternut uniform of the 8th Virginia Infantry out on the table. I couldn't help but notice how the color drained from Olivia's face at the sight of that uniform and what she knew it meant. Only Conor was thrilled and immediately wanted to know if he could try on the jacket. He ran his fingers longingly across the metal buttons. The desire in his eyes was unmistakable.

"I done re-enlisted with my old unit," announced Pa. "The Army of Northern Virginia needs men badly. President Jefferson Davis upped the age limit for enlistment in order to get more recruits. My shoulder has healed as well as it's gonna, and I got no excuse not to go. I know I said I'd never do this to y'all again, but I'm needed and a man's gotta do what he believes is right. With Conor here now, y'all will do just fine. The 8th is headin' this way from Winchester, and then I'll join up with them."

★ ★ ★

Jessie looked over at me, and I could see the fear in her gray-blue eyes. The last time Pa had gone off like this meant only sorrow for us. She held Garrett's little hand and I saw her lower lip quiver, but she fought back her tears. Olivia said nothing, as she quietly began to set the table for supper. But when she turned to stir the stew, I saw a tear glimmer in the firelight as it fell from her cheek. She quickly brushed her cheek with the back of her hand, and I don't think anyone else noticed. I was sure she was thinking that she'd already lost one husband to the war, and now she was going to send off another. Jessie and I had lost our mother and watched our father suffer from a Yankee bullet. None of us wanted to make such sacrifices again.

Dinner would have been very quiet that night except for Conor's constant stream of questions to Pa about the war, the battles, and the 8th.

"What was happenin' in town, Uncle Nate? Were there troops there?"

"Every available buildin' in town is bein' used to care for the wounded Confederates from Manassas. I'm mighty glad that Olivia and Garrett are out here with us now," Pa replied. "By mid-September most of our able-bodied troops moved on up to Maryland to a town called Sharpsburg near Antietam Creek."

"What happened there, Uncle Nate?" Conor pressed.

"There was some fierce fightin'. Things didn't go well for General Lee and our boys." Pa paused a minute as if thinking about what to say next. "Fortunately, they were able to slip back into Virginia before the Union troops knew that they had gone." Pa sensed that this conversation was not sitting

★ ★ ★

well with the rest of us, and he tried to answer Conor's questions carefully so as not to give us any more cause for alarm than we already had.

Conor would have continued pressing Pa endlessly about the war had not Olivia very quietly, but very curtly, said, "Conor, I do believe we've heard more than enough of war for one mealtime. Kindly hush now, and leave Nate to eat in peace." Conor knew better than to argue when his sister used that tone of voice.

22
Emancipation Proclamation, September 22, 1862

After dinner, Pa and Conor and I went out to the porch and he told us what else he had learned in town. "Boys, that battle at Antietam Creek was a disaster. More men were killed that day in a single cornfield than anyone could begin to count. It was our first defeat. Fortunately, the 8th had only a handful of men there. Many of our boys had just had enough fightin' and took the opportunity to spend time with their families when they passed so close to home, like the two stragglers who came through here. As those two said, our Southern boys didn't want to be the aggressors. They were fightin' to protect their homes, not to invade someone else's.

"After that so-called Union victory," he continued, "President Lincoln decided this would be a good time to announce a new proclamation. What he said was as of January 1, 1863, slaves in all states that were still fightin' agin' the Union, would be free. The Federal troops would not do a thin' to keep the slaves from anythin' they might do to git their freedom.

★ ★ ★

★ ★ ★

They are callin' it the Emancipation Proclamation, 'cause emancipation means bein' set free. Needless to say, that news isn't settin' well with slave owners in these parts and, of course, by the slave owners way down South. For farmers like us who have no slaves, it really don't mean much. But we're all wonderin' what effect that proclamation might have on the course of this here war."

As I listened to Pa and thought about Lincoln's words, I remembered James Robinson, who had helped Jessie and me. Though he had been given his freedom, he had spent years trying to earn enough money to buy his wife's and his children's freedom. This proclamation could mean that they would all be free as of January first. For Jim's sake and for his family, I hoped it was true.

Pa stood before us a few days later fully clothed in his woolen butternut uniform. With his gear draped across his shoulders and brass buttons polished, we couldn't help but feel a glow of pride. Seeing his old black felt hat perched on his blond head, and his gun in hand, I almost forgot for a moment how close we had come to losing him the last time he went off to fight. Pa stepped forward and hugged each of us in turn, finally clasping Olivia to him and vowing that no Union force was strong enough to keep him from returning home to the family he loved. Then once again, we watched until he disappeared from our sight on his way to join the 8th, now a part of Pickett's brigade.

23
Letters from Pa

That fall and winter of 1863 were long and dreary.

★ ★ ★

Occasionally, Pa would manage to get a letter to us. We would all gather around as Olivia read them aloud. She would re-read that one each evening until a new letter arrived to take its place.

Pa went on from Culpeper to Fredericksburg where he stayed until February. His letters from there told us of the battle on Marye's Heights. The 8th, he assured us, was safely positioned. They watched as wave after wave of Yankees, under General Burnside, crossed an open field trying to get at our Confederate units. Our troops were entrenched behind a stone wall at the top of the hill. The Yankees didn't stand a chance. He wrote that someone had heard General Lee say that day as he watched the fighting below, "It is well that war is so terrible or we should grow too fond of it." Pa agreed with him, and continued to hope this all would soon end.

His next letter informed us that he and the 8th were headed for North Carolina to gather more supplies for the Army. We worried to hear he was going so far away, but soon another letter arrived to say that they were back in Virginia still collecting "hogs and hominy for the Army," as he put it.

He wrote a brief note to us as the 8th rejoined Lee's forces near Culpeper. He said that General Thomas Stonewall Jackson had been shot at Chancellorsville and died. The worst part was that he was shot by one of our own Confederate soldiers. General Lee said he felt as though he had lost his right arm when he lost Stonewall. Pa said General Lee was moving them north, and everyone was sure that this would be the last big battle of the war.

We didn't know then, but found out later that they were headed to Pennsylvania to a place called Gettysburg. Pa's

★ ★ ★

letters stopped coming after that. We eventually heard that the South had been defeated at Gettysburg. Beaten soundly. We didn't know what to think. Olivia wouldn't let us utter any bad thoughts. She said she just knew that Pa was all right.

At long last, we received a short note from Pa. All it said was, "I'm alive and well. We're headed back to Richmond."

24
An Unexpected Visit, 1864

Fall became winter, and winter turned to spring. Letters from Pa had been few and far between. Our life went on as always, working at the farm, eking out our meager existence. Times were tough for everyone.

Then one mild March morning Olivia was sitting quietly spinning her wool into yarn. The gentle whirr of the wheel was the only sound in the house. She lifted her eyes and glanced out the window as she worked. A man was approaching on the road. No one else had seen him. Olivia stood up, knocking her spinning wheel over, and sending her basket of wool flying across the floor. Before any of us had time to realize what was happening, she was out the door crying and laughing and babbling outloud, "It's Nate! It's Nate! He's come home to us!"

When we heard that, we all dropped what we were doing and ran after her. By the time we got down the road, Olivia and Pa were already in each other's arms. Jessie, now almost eleven, was torn between running like a child and trying to be a young lady. But when she reached Pa, she threw her arms up around his neck and let herself be swept off the ground and twirled around. Garrett was the last one down the road,

★ ★ ★

running as fast as his little legs would take him. Pa bent down and caught him up in a flying leap. Conor and I held back, trying our best to appear the strong young men we were expected to be. Pa reached out and gave us each a good old bear hug, then with smiles all around, our reunited family walked arm in arm back to the house. It had been a year and a half since Pa had left us.

That night our house was jubilant such as it hadn't been in some time. Olivia even managed to prepare a feast of sorts from one of the hams she had been saving for just such an occasion. Pa was home, even if it was only for a few days. He looked much thinner than when he had left, and his gray-blue eyes had a hollow, somber look to them.

★ ★ ★

"Our unit is encamped somewhat comfortably in some log cabins we put together on the North James River. We're there as part of the defenses for Richmond," Pa told us at dinner. "Since things've been sort of calm for awhile, many of us were given a bit of leave. Our commanders decided it was better to give us leave than to have us desert. I'm sure glad they did. It's good to be home, even for just a short spell."

That evening as the sun set in a blaze of pink over the Blue Ridge Mountains, Pa sat on the front porch and told Conor and me all about Gettysburg. His voice began to quaver as he described the bravery and courage of their commanders. He recounted watching as his own brigade commander, General Garnett, was shot right out of his saddle. Following this, General Armistead led a determined charge across the open field, his hat held high upon his sword for all of his men to see. Armistead and his brigade moved through the 8th's already decimated brigade. On the other side of that field, the Yankees, entrenched behind a stone wall, picked them off like rabbits on the run. Armistead advanced only to be mortally wounded for his effort. Pa's eyes brimmed with tears as he described the futility of their actions that day.

He looked right at me and said, "Remember that day at Manassas. This was ten times worse and this time we were not the victors. I don't know how I managed to survive the slaughter that followed. Somehow a few of us helped each other back to where we started. And then like dogs with our tails between our legs, we limped back into Virginia. We had gone north with such great hopes, only to be bitterly defeated. We lost so many men from our unit. Other brigades lost almost all of theirs. Many were taken prisoner. The conscripts

★ ★ ★

we have comin' in now to replace the men we lost just don't have the same desire or spark. Our forces are dwindlin'. I don't know what will become of us. But we must remain true to our cause until all of this somehow ends. Our main goal now is to protect Richmond and President Davis."

Later that evening, Pa and Olivia sat rocking on the porch in the dark as Conor and I went to bed. We kept reliving all the details of the war that Pa had described to us. We were young and eager and thrilled by the adventure that war and fighting seemed to hold. We were able to look past the gore and see only the glory.

Pa's time at home went by all too quickly and soon he had to return to Richmond. Once again he repeated those familiar, but worn out words, "I don't think this can go on much longer. Just try to hold on. I know it's difficult. But we will make it."

25
Two New Soldiers, 1864

After that unexpected visit, Conor and I lived to hear any news from Pa. We talked endlessly together about the fighting and the war. We boasted that we would be ten times braver and better than those weak scraggly conscripts that Pa had told us about. The more we talked, the braver and bolder we became.

So one day Conor said to me, "I have an idea how we can help both Pa and the South." He explained that Lee was leading a good fight, but he needed more men. He said, "I think we oughta go and join Lee's army. You know how we both

★ ★ ★

agree that we'd be better soldiers than half them conscripts they got."

"But Conor," I said, "we ain't old enough."

And he replied, "Don't worry. I got a plan"

One morning, a few days later, instead of going to the fields, we snuck off to Warrenton. I suppose I didn't really think we'd have much chance of enlisting because of our age, or I might have put up more of an argument. I just thought going to town and trying to enlist would be something exciting to do for a change.

When we got to the courthouse, Conor pulled me aside before we went in and gave me a tiny scrap of paper with the number eighteen written on it. "Take off your boot and stick this inside," he told me, and he did the same. "Just let me do the talkin' and do whatever I do," he said.

Once inside, he told the man, we want to sign on to fight. The man looked us both over kind of funny-like, and then he asked, "You boys over eighteen? You gotta be over eighteen to sign up."

Now Conor, he stood up straight and tall and said right out to that man, "Yessir, I am *over* eighteen."

He nudged me and I stepped up and just like him I said, "Yessir, I am *over* eighteen, too."

After we signed the papers and walked out, Conor said, "See how easy that was, and we didn't have to lie. We really was *over* eighteen, even if we were only over the number eighteen on a piece of paper."

As it turned out, that was the easy part. Conor, as usual, was good at getting us into predicaments and this one was really serious. At this point in the war, the Confederate forces

★ ★ ★

needed men so badly they would have taken anyone who could take a breath. Before I fully realized what I had done, we were on our way to join up with Lee's forces near Richmond and, hopefully, with Pa.

Although I was excited with the thought of being in Pa's unit and helping end this war, I felt terribly guilty about how we left Jessie and Garrett and my stepmother alone. Neither of us was brave enough to tell Olivia or Jessie to their face what we had done. Instead we wrote them a letter and left it on the table. We snuck off before dawn like thieves into the night. I couldn't believe I had actually done this, but I had to admit I felt a tremendous thrill of excitement as we headed south.

26
Reunited With Pa

That was July of '64. From then on things didn't go the way we thought they would. Being a soldier held none of the glory we had imagined. We spent hours slogging through mud and rain, or tramping through dust and heat. Our food, what little there was of it, was terrible. Graybacks, as the wretched body lice were called, invaded every inch of our clothing and bodies. We didn't even have complete uniforms. We wore what we brought from home. Many men salvaged uniforms and boots from those who didn't make it on the battlefield.

Pa and the 8th had gone on to Cold Harbor in the beginning of June. When we finally caught up with them, they were entrenched between Richmond and Petersburg. Conor and I were overjoyed when we spotted Pa across the camp.

★ ★ ★

We were sure he would be thrilled to see us ready to fight at his side. But Pa immediately remembered the last time I came to find him in the midst of battle. He feared the worst about Olivia. When we finally assured him that Olivia, Jessie, and Garrett were well when we last saw them in July, he seemed relieved. Then his relief quickly turned into rage, and he began to yell at us, "How could you two be so inconsiderate, leaving a woman and two children alone to fend for themselves? I counted on you to take care of them in my place while I was gone. And how, *how* could you go off and leave Olivia in her present condition?" He was beside himself.

Conor and I gave each other a puzzled look. "Condition? What condition?" I finally managed to mumble.

Seeing the confused look on our faces, he said, "Didn't you know Olivia is goin' to have a baby? She sent me a letter not too long ago tellin' me the good news. She thought the baby would be born sometime in December."

"Pa, we never knew. Olivia never said anythin' to us. She was doin' everythin' just like she always done. You know we never woulda left if she had told us," I muttered numbly. Conor stood with a look of utter disbelief on his face. For once he was completely speechless.

I never felt so low as I did at that moment. I realized that once again I had let my pa down when he needed me. Conor and I thought that Pa and the South needed us here to fight. Now it was too late to turn back and undo what we had done. Pa was more upset than I'd ever seen him; I wasn't sure if he would ever forgive us. Only the impending threat of an attack by Union forces on Richmond made Pa shift his focus to that and away from his anger at us.

★ ★ ★

★ ★ ★

Mail was very erratic now, and we could only hope that Olivia and Jessie and Garrett were managing alone. Our Confederate lines were faced with ever strengthening Union forces, which were closing in on us and Richmond.

For Conor and me, being on the front lines meant we were now hearing war reports first hand, and much of the news we were hearing was not good. We knew that Lincoln was re-elected and that General Sherman was marching through Georgia, burning everything in his path.

When January came, we welcomed in the new year from our camp on the James River south of Richmond. Everyone hoped 1865 would bring an end to this war. It was difficult to see how it could continue on much longer. Yankee forces kept pounding away at us. With Lincoln's Inauguration in March came a renewed determination on their part to restore the Union and free the slaves. That had become their battle cry.

27
Fighting to Sayler's Creek

Conor and I realized that all our visions of heroism and glory were just that—visions. Reality was much more dismal. Pa resigned himself to the fact that we were now soldiers. We heard no news from home. We all thought about Olivia and the baby and knew that it should have been born by now. Not one of us dared to say anything out loud. We each hoped and prayed to ourselves that all had gone well.

Toward the end of March we were sent to the depot in Richmond, and trains took us from there to Petersburg. Then

★ ★ ★

we slogged on through the mud to join up with General Lee. Conor and I were finally going to get to see some real fighting. The streams were swollen with cold spring rains and many of the bridges had washed away. In spite of the harsh conditions, we advanced on the Yankees. Our 8th regiment, part of the brigade commanded by the now General Hunton, had the Yanks backed up against Gravelly Run. Then we made the mistake of letting up briefly to regroup, flushed with victory. For a very short moment, Conor and I actually believed the South could still be victorious. However, we were quickly jerked back to reality as the Federal forces counterattacked, and that night we ended up in the mud right where we had started.

Shortly after that, General Hunton was informed that Pickett's forces had collapsed at Five Forks. We were sent there to help reinforce their dwindling line, only to be pressed on again all that afternoon and night toward the Southside Railroad. We'd been on the march for over twenty-four hours without rest or food. We could hardly move as our feet and boots stuck in the cold clay muck. Conor said it looked like we were retreating. I had no idea where we were going. I just knew we were all getting mighty tired and hungry. Somehow though, we managed to get to Pickett's division just outside of a place called Amelia. We still had not rested or eaten. Someone managed to scrounge up a measley ear of dried corn for each of us. We tried to grind the hard kernels with our teeth as we marched. Conor, Pa and I hung onto each other, holding each other up. The Yankees were breathing down our necks. Hungry and tired beyond belief, we finally reached Sayler's Creek. The three of us had been able to stay together

★ ★ ★

until then, but that was when it became obvious that we were outnumbered and the scrambling began. That was April 6th. And that was the day I was captured.

28
Point Lookout Prison, Maryland, 1865

The Confederate troops left behind in Richmond were forced to surrender the capital city on April 3rd, three days before our defeat at Sayler's Creek. Many of those men captured in Richmond were sent to Point Lookout Prison, a 23-acre triangle of Maryland swamp formed by the Potomac River and the Chesapeake Bay. The Union Army decided this would be an ideal place for a prison and established it originally for all the prisoners they had captured at Gettysburg. Sealed off by water on two sides and a swamp on the third, Point Lookout was certainly vile enough to be a prison and was crowded beyond its limits.

Then as we, Lee's Army of Northern Virginia, began our retreat, struggling desperately to fight our way toward Appomattox, thousands more of us Rebs were captured and sent to Point Lookout. Such was my fate. Captured! The word still seems unbelievable to me. Actually, surrendered seemed a better word. Still, not much glory or honor in either.

I realized very quickly that all the grim tales that had been told by one Confederate soldier to another about Point Lookout had been true. Those prisoners fortunate enough to have been released or exchanged from there quickly spread the word of its horrendous conditions. Now time had only aggravated what had already been unbearable. The number

★ ★ ★

of prisoners held within these walls was far beyond reason and conditions were inhumane.

I could now only wonder what had become of Pa and Conor. I asked and searched for them all the way to Point Lookout. They hadn't been among the many prisoners taken on that terrible 'Black Thursday of the Confederacy'. On that fateful day, Major Berkeley, Commander of the 8th, realized what a hopeless situation we were in, as Union soldiers surged in on us from all sides. At that moment, he made the decision to release the few remaining men of the 8th. His last order urged us to escape in any way we could. Such an order meant that this was the end of the 8th Virginia Regiment. But there was no time to think about that. The last I saw of Pa and Conor was them running ahead of me toward the trees. The Yankees were coming from all directions. I got cut off. Nowhere to run. Conor yelled back to me, "This way, Jacob!" But then I tripped and fell, and that Yankee private, looking as muddy and cold and frightened as I was, had shoved the tip of his rifle into my back. Like so many others that day who were worn out and starving, I surrendered. I had tried to look around for Pa's curly blond head or Conor's dark hair, to no avail. Had they been captured? Had they made it to safety? Or were they dead in some cold muddy ditch? I wanted to believe that they were all right. If I believed that, I knew I could endure this. Someday, I vowed, I would go home from this place. I would go home to the waiting arms of my family. That thought, and that thought alone, gave me the strength to face being at Point Lookout.

'Black Thursday' was the name the Confederates gave to April 6, 1865. All of us weary Confederate prisoners captured

★ ★ ★

that day had been marched along red clay roads made slick by spring rains. Yankee soldiers prodded and herded us like so many cattle onto cramped and suffocating railroad cars headed for the City Point docks. From there we were transferred to crowded steamers, which took us down the James River and then up the Chesapeake Bay to this dismal prison. Some Rebs never made it, dying along the way of wounds, starvation, or just sheer exhaustion. Perhaps they were the fortunate ones to have been spared the ordeal of Point Lookout.

Our wretched detachment of Confederates finally docked at a weatherbeaten wharf jutting into the Potomac. We were herded off the boat by blue uniformed soldiers jabbing us in the back with their rifles as we trudged down the narrow gangplank.

"Hurry up there, Rebs. Keep moving. Gotta get this steamer unloaded and back on its way. You're gonna love your new home here at Point Lookout," one old guard had jeered, chuckling at his own joke. None of us seemed to think it was funny.

A skinny red-haired prisoner in front of me stumbled and fell. "Get up, you Reb. Keep moving!" growled another guard. I helped the fallen man to his feet before the guard could hit him with his rifle butt.

As we stumbled along, another guard shouted, "Hey, Johnny Reb! Whatcha gonna do now that your old Lee has surrendered to General Grant at Appomattox? You boys shoulda known better'n to fight agin' the United States of America. We've got you Rebs whupped now!"

So it *was* true! There had been rumors along the way about

★ ★ ★

Lee's surrender. We thought it was just a Yankee trick to beat our spirits down even more than they already had been. But I knew that if what had happened to us at Sayler's Creek was any example of the remaining battles, Lee's defeat was definitely possible. Still and all, I didn't want to believe it. Because if it was true, then I had even more reason to be concerned about the fate of Pa and Conor.

"Your name, rank, and where you're from, soldier," demanded a dark-skinned Yankee guard at the end of the wharf.

"Jacob Harding, Private. Virginia," I replied and was shuffled along to the next station.

29
Good Friday, 1865

Settling in at Point Lookout didn't take much effort. All I had were the few meager belongings I carried on my back, nothing more, nothing less. No one else had much either. Everyone here had only one goal: to survive until the day came when we would be able to go back home.

I was assigned to a tent already filled to capacity with other prisoners. But then every tent was overcrowded. I overheard two of the men sitting in the tent say that this was Good Friday and that Sunday would be Easter. I thought to myself, "What a joke! This is definitely not a *good* Friday for me."

I looked around, surveying the prison grounds. Before me stretched an endless sea of tattered, dirty tents. Along the far west wall of the prison yard there were five wooden cookhouses. That was where we would get the few miserable scraps allotted to us each day. Penning us in on all sides was

★ ★ ★

a towering 14-foot high wooden fence. Armed guards moved back and forth at all times along a catwalk high up on the outside of the wall. The guards could see and be seen from all angles. They watched like vultures from this lofty perch as if daring the prisoners below to cross over the "deadline." The deadline was the first thing I had been warned about when I came into Point Lookout. The deadline was a ditch parallel to the fence and a few feet away from it. Any prisoner trying to cross that ditch would be shot, and those vultures up there seemed to be just itching for someone to try. I was not going to give them that opportunity if I could help it. I wondered to myself, how long I would be here. A month? A year? A lifetime?

The next morning, I awoke to a lot of commotion. A rumor was going through the prison like wildfire. The men were saying President Lincoln was shot last night while attending a play in Washington. He never regained consciousness and died that very morning. I thought to myself, *Lincoln was assassinated on Good Friday, the very same Good Friday that I had declared had not been good for me. Now it had also not been good for the President of the Union.* We prisoners knew the rumor must be true because the guards walked around dazed and stunned that day, some even with tears in their eyes. I wondered what effect Lincoln's death would have on this war. What would become of the South now that Lincoln was dead and Lee had surrendered? We heard that fighting was still going on in some parts of the South. General Johnston had still not surrendered his Southern forces to General Grant. How long would it all continue and what would become of those of us at Point Lookout?

★ ★ ★

30
Miserable Days and Nights

Prison life was meant to be dismal, and it was. Living at the water's edge meant it was always damp and humid. The boundary waters on each side of the camp were brackish, or slightly salty, and not fit to drink. But they wouldn't have been drinkable anyway, since most of the filth from the prison drained into the bay and the river, polluting it. When a storm or especially high tide came, much of our camp space was flooded. These times were particularly miserable.

Bugs swarmed constantly around my bare ankles. I guess my trousers had trouble keeping up with the growing I had done this last year. The flies competed with the mosquitos to see who could torture me the most. Unfortunately, the mosquitos with their painful piercing bites won every time. The only joy Rebs like me got was that the mosquitoes bit the Yankee guards as fiercely as they bit us. But the guards had better clothes for protection. The mosquito was king at Point Lookout.

We were rousted out of our tents every morning by a blaring bugle for roll call. The same roll call was repeated again at sundown to be sure none of us had escaped. Such tasks were hurriedly accomplished just so the guards could say they had been done. After that it was up to each prisoner to figure out how to while away the long hours in between. Some men simply withdrew from everyone and tried to sleep the time away. However, I soon learned that many of the men possessed a keen determination to survive against all odds. I was constantly amazed at the ingenuity of many prisoners as they

★ ★ ★

used every cunning or skill they had to try to improve their meager existence.

Anyone who had some money or found a way to earn it could find ways to buy additional scraps of food or other items that might improve life just a bit. Some prisoners had developed clever ways to make items to sell, such as carving bits of bone or wood into rings or games. These pursuits also helped to pass away the long and seemingly endless hours. Some made "coffee" of sorts from stale bread crumbs they collected and toasted to a dark brown. Others caught fish or crabs and sold or traded the extras that they didn't eat themselves. Food was so meager that even rats trapped at night were cooked or sold. Anything could be used for barter, and some items were so well made even the Union guards wanted to buy them. The guards had access to things from outside the prison walls, and so their trade was very desirable. Some prisoners were lucky enough to receive some mail, and even an occasional package. This also provided additional supplies for trade or barter.

Of course, there were always a few who tried to steal what they didn't have. Prison punishment was swift for those who were caught. The thief was fitted with a 'wooden jacket' made from a barrel without a bottom and with a hole cut in the top just large enough for his head to fit through. Wearing this 'wooden jacket' rendered the guilty man's hands completely useless. Now he not only couldn't steal, but he also couldn't do anything else either. It was often a deadly punishment.

Mealtime, if it could be called that, was something to be tolerated in order to survive. Some of the prisoners had been

★ ★ ★

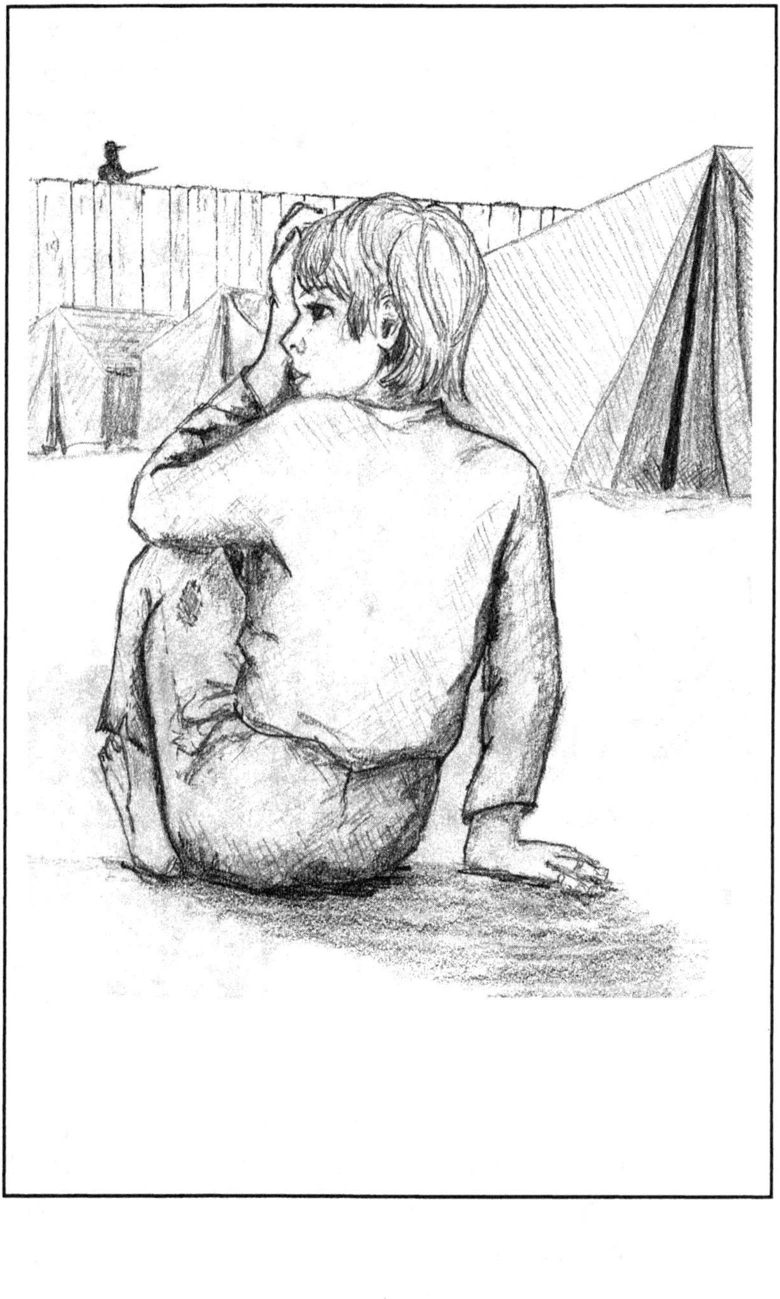

★ ★ ★

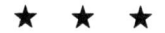

here a long time. As they waited in line, their glazed eyes and emaciated bodies were evidence of the hardships they had endured. Many were clad in shirts and pants so worn and threadbare that their skin showed through. Some had tried sewing on patches, but it hardly seemed worth the effort. Most were barefoot, having long ago worn out boots marching over endless, dusty roads.

Arriving at the head of the line, a pot-bellied Union guard plopped a ladleful of lukewarm liquid into our outstretched cups. He called it soup, but it looked more like gray washwater. Considering the guard's size and shape, it was obvious that he and the rest of the Union troops had a much better menu than we did. I wouldn't look into my cup. I closed my eyes and quickly gulped down its contents, trying not to taste it. Once I did look and saw a greasy glob of gray fat floating on the surface. As the slimy fat slid down my throat, I thought back to the wonderful smoked hams and bacon I used to eat at the farm. What I wouldn't have given for a piece of that ham then, ham and bacon that Pa used to prepare. I knew Jessie and I had promised never to eat ham or bacon again because of Squealer. But, at Point Lookout Prison, I would have broken that promise in a heartbeat. How I would have cherished a piece of Squealer's delicious ham or bacon at that very moment.

The nights at Point Lookout were the worst. The tents were crowded beyond capacity, the blankets dirty and ragged, if you had one at all, and all sorts of vermin shared them with you. I never realized how many despicable creatures could afflict a man. Soldiers on the march were plagued not only with a lack of food and water, but with an abundance of dirt,

★ ★ ★

lice, and other vermin. Each night I would dream about Ma's or Olivia's delicious meals. I even dreamed about taking a bath in a barrelful of hot water with lye soap. I never thought I'd ever hear myself say that, but I would have done anything to rid myself of the crawly 'varmints' that bit and itched me every day. As if that wasn't enough, the flies and mosquitos added to the misery. Sleep never came easy. If the vermin didn't keep me awake, the hunger pangs in my stomach did. Some nights it was all I could do to keep from crying out with the pain. Other nights I'd lie awake listening to the faceless wails and moans of others in the hot, humid darkness.

In those overcrowded conditions, it was hard to find a place to be alone. Sometimes, though, I wanted to be by myself to think and dream. In my daydreams I could escape from those prison walls. Looking back, things in the past didn't seem as bad and time seemed to go by a little faster. I'd pull my knees up tight against my chest and wrap my arms around my ankles to protect them. My tangled hair shielded my face as I rested my head on my knees. As prisoners, time was the only thing that had not been taken away from us. And here time seemed endless. What day was it? I didn't really know. Dates and time didn't really mean much. One day was just like another. Same routine, same misery. Wake up to roll call in the morning. Endless day. Meager food. Roll call at night. Go to sleep. How I wished I was anywhere but there.

Yet despite all of this, there was a determination not only to survive, but also to maintain a sense of pride and loyalty to the cause. Any of us could have taken the easy way out of those prison walls. Any prisoner who was willing to swear an oath of loyalty to the Union and agree to go out to the

★ ★ ★

Western frontier and fight against the Indians could walk out of those walls immediately. Put on that dark blue uniform. Fight out West for the Union. That's all. Yet very few Rebs had given in and done that. Most would rather have died there than be disloyal to the cause. Such fierce loyalty never ceased to amaze me.

31
The South Surrenders, May, 1865

Rumors always flew through the prison. We heard General Johnston had finally surrendered to Grant in North Carolina. And then on May 10th, the guards gleefully announced that Jefferson Davis, President of the Confederate States of America, had been captured in Georgia. On that day, Andrew Johnson, who became the Union President after Lincoln's assassination, issued a proclamation that declared the armed resistance of the Southern States was at an end.

We had mixed emotions when we heard that news. We were thankful that the end of the fighting had finally come and the hope that we might soon be released seemed to pick up everyone's spirits. But proud men always find it hard to accept defeat. As prisoners of war, we wondered what our fate would be now that the war was officially over. No one had an answer for us, and our dismal routine at Point Lookout continued as if there had been no proclamation at all. June came, and there was still no word as to what would become of us. How much longer was this all going to drag on?

Finally the words that we had all been waiting for were announced. On June 6, 1865, President Johnson declared that

★ ★ ★

all Confederate prisoners who were willing to take an oath of allegiance would be released. Point Lookout Prison officials began making preparations to put this into effect as soon as possible. All around the camp there were shouts and cheers of relief and joy with the prospects of our impending release.

Over the course of the next few weeks, prisoners were systematically released. With tens of thousands of prisoners locked up there, the process was painfully slow. As required, each prisoner had to repeat the oath of allegiance to the United States of America, and then each was allowed to board a steamboat that would start his journey home.

I had to wait for almost two weeks before my name was finally called. I thought that day would never come. And so it was, that on Wednesday, June 14, 1865, I repeated the oath of allegiance to the Union. As I did, I thought of all that had happened to me up to this point in my life. I didn't have the difficulty uttering the words to that oath that some of the other prisoners had seemed to have. I'd had reservations and concerns about this war from the very beginning. With my right hand raised, I swore "henceforth to fully support, protect, and defend the Constitution of the United States of America and to abide by its laws." That done, I was able to march with the others onto a steamboat headed up the Potomac River for the docks at Alexandria and home.

32
Heading for Home

A motley, ragged, emaciated group of prisoners stood beside me at the rail of the boat. Once there had only been

★ ★ ★

depression and despair visible in their eyes, but now a gleam of determination and hope flickered through their anguish. Soon they would be reunited with loved ones they hadn't seen for years. In the back of many of their minds was the fear that perhaps no one was left waiting for them. I wouldn't even let myself think such depressing thoughts. As I stared out over the shimmering water of the Potomac I thought about my home. I couldn't wait to get to Virginia again. Home. The thought of it made me shiver all over with anticipation. Soon. Soon. The churning water seemed to pick up that word and say it with me. Soon. Soon. Soon.

The steamer inched upriver with agonizing slowness. I watched as forests of dogwoods, redbuds, and hollies passed by on my left. The forests of Virginia. My Virginia. So close. I could still hear the boat chanting, "Soon. Soon. Soon."

The city of Alexandria appeared at last framed in the glow of a glorious setting sun. With anxious faces, all of us watched and waited intently as the distance between us and the docks diminished. A collective sigh of relief went up when the steamer finally banged up against the dock and the heavy ropes were secured to their moorings.

Everyone began to jostle and push in their rush to disembark. Forced to wait and suffer in silence for so long within the dismal walls of Point Lookout, their patience had worn out. A few like myself had only waited months, but some had waited for years for this moment. There was an exuberant crush of bodies as we shoved one another to race down the gangplank and reach home soil. This was the moment we had all been dreaming about. There was confusion at first, but eventually everyone collected themselves into groups

★ ★ ★

headed for various towns and cities. Some men shook hands, some clapped each other joyfully on the back, and others hugged one another unabashedly in the dimming purple twilight. Then everyone shuffled off, headed for various depots in hopes that there would be trains ready to take them home by the fastest and most direct routes.

I looked for the old Orange and Alexandria line which I knew went right to Catlett Station, the very same station where Conor and I had watched Stuart's raid almost three years ago and thought that might be as close as we would ever get to the war. Oh, how I wish that had been true. Hard to believe so much time had passed since then. I hoped the trains were running and not overcrowded. I knew with luck I could be on my way home that night. Oh, how good that sounded.

I found myself surrounded by a whole contingent of men, all newly sworn to protect and uphold the United States Constitution, waiting at the depot for a train to take them to Manassas Junction, to Catlett and then on to Culpeper, Gordonsville, Charlottesville and points south. We climbed aboard, filling the cars with noisy anticipation. Riding through the night, everyone reminisced, always with some fear and trepidation. Would their farms and homes still be intact? Would the loved ones that they left behind, and longed for all this time, still be waiting for them? Would they still be alive?

A big group got off at Manassas Junction. My heart began to race. Only a couple more stops and it would be my turn. My heart was beating so fast I thought it would explode before I got there. Then someone called out, "Catlett Station! All those for Catlett Station!"

★ ★ ★

33
The Last Two Miles

It was still dark when I stepped off the train. A touch of pink was beginning to creep into the eastern sky. I took a deep breath. Oh, how good freedom smelled.

Home was about two miles or so, due north. In the first darkness of the morning I hadn't really been able to see. I'd been too caught up in the excitement of being so close to home. But as the sun gradually rose in the sky, I saw the devastation of the war all around me. Along the rail line and stretching out for as far as I could see, there was not a tree left standing. Most of the fences had been cut or torn down, all probably used for firewood for the Union forces that passed through. Farm fields, once rich and lush, were unplowed and overgrown with weeds. I started to walk faster even though I'd been going without sleep for over 24 hours now. I was afraid to think about the condition of our farm. I was afraid to think about where my family was.

Visions of Jessie and Olivia and Garrett raced through my mind. Oh, dear Lord, please let them have come through those difficult times by themselves. I never should have left them. How could I ever face Pa if anything had happened to them after we left? I still had to believe that Pa and Conor had gotten away safely that day at Sayler's Creek. Oh, I had never had a moment of doubt before. Why am I so afraid now when I am so close?

I began to run. My heart pounded like a drum and I gasped for breath. Then, as I turned down the rutted lane leading to our farm, I stopped dead in my tracks. Though I had seen

★ ★ ★

devastation so many other places during this war, I wasn't prepared to see it here at home. In the distance I could make out the silhouette of our house, still standing, but all of our fences were gone as well as most of the lovely old trees that had made this place so special. I moved as if in a trance. As I approached the house, I could see that the war had taken its toll there, too. It looked sadly neglected and forlorn. Wasn't there anyone home to take care of it? It was some relief when I noticed thin wisps of smoke rising from the chimney. Someone was there! I strained my eyes, hoping to see anyone or anything that was familiar. But it was very early. Just then a young woman stepped outside to pick up a few pieces of firewood. As she bent down, I saw her blond hair glowing in the early morning sun, and I knew it wasn't Olivia. Who was this strange woman in my house? I moved even more slowly now, not knowing what to expect. The young woman stopped and looked my way when she heard my footsteps. Startled, she was about to go back into the house. But then she hesitated ever so briefly, and squinted in my direction. Then she set down the firewood, never taking her eyes off of me. She started to walk towards me, slowly at first, until suddenly, she broke into a run, crying out, "Jacob? Jacob, is that you? Is it really you at last?"

And before we knew it, we were hugging and kissing and crying in the middle of the road. We were both talking at the same time, and we had no idea what each of us was saying nor did we care.

Finally I held her off at arms length and exclaimed, "My, oh my! Jessie, you've done growed up, little sister!" She blushed as she tucked her arm into mine and we headed toward the house.

★ ★ ★

Conor came out just then, pulling up his suspenders. He only needed to take one look at Jessie and the young man with her, before he yelled wildly into the house, "It's Jacob! Jacob's home! I do declare, my cousin's finally come home."

Afterwards I couldn't recall who had gotten to me next and who all I'd hugged. I only knew that I was surrounded by arms and tears and cries of joy and thanks. I was so grateful to be home. I didn't even remember when Pa picked me up and carried me into the house when my legs finally collapsed. I scarcely remembered eating the warm porridge that Olivia gave me before I fell into the first deep, comfortable sleep I'd had in over a year.

When I eventually opened my eyes, Jessie and Conor were both sitting beside my bed. "I thought you'd never wake up," Conor laughed. "We thought you were goin' to sleep your life away."

"Don't tease him, Conor. He needs his rest and he needs to eat. Look how thin he is. If he were any skinnier, he'd fall between the cracks in the floor. Olivia and I are goin' to have to do some serious cookin' for this boy."

At twelve, Jessie was becoming a beautiful young woman. Her long blond curls were pulled back at each side of her head and her blue eyes sparkled through thick, curly lashes. She was definitely not the little sister I'd left behind.

Olivia and Pa came over to the bed when they heard us talking. A shy, six-year-old Garrett was peering out at me from behind his mother's skirt. But the best sight to my eyes was the chubby-cheeked baby in Olivia's arms. Olivia lay the baby on the bed next to me. "This is your little sister,

★ ★ ★

Annie. She was our blessed Christmas present. She's been waitin' for a long time to meet her big brother."

I snuggled the gurgling baby in my arms. All my prayers and hopes had been answered. I touched my lips to the baby's soft cheeks and peach fuzz hair. How lucky could one person be? I was the happiest person in the world at that moment.

★ ★ ★

34
Picking Up the Pieces

That night as the whole Harding family sat at the table holding hands, Pa bowed his head and prayed, "Thank you, Lord, for safely bringing home all the men in this family from this difficult and trying war. Thank you, Lord, for watching over my dear Olivia through these troublesome times. Thank you, Lord, for protecting Jessie and Garrett and little Annie, who fill our lives with great joy. For all that you have given us, we thank you, Lord. Amen."

Pa had never been much of a religious man, but I learned first hand what war can do to change a man. Pa's prayer was deeply touching to me. There was so much that our family had to be thankful for. And there was so much that we needed to catch up on as we feasted on the meal that Olivia and Jessie had prepared for this joyous occasion.

Pa went first to explain to me what happened to him that day at Sayler's Creek. "I was one of the fortunate ones who was able to run and hide without gettin' caught. I never saw what happened to you or Conor in all the confusion. There were two other men with me and not one of us hesitated when the order came that day to escape in any way we could. We headed north, with only one thought in our minds. We had fought enough. We had nothin' more to give to the cause. It was time to go home and make peace. I needed to get home to my family. And that is exactly what I did as quickly as I could."

Conor's experiences that day had taken him in another direction. When he was separated from Pa and me, he followed another small group of soldiers as they struggled toward

★ ★ ★

Appomattox. There he witnessed the final humiliation and surrender of General Robert E. Lee. Conor's eyes brimmed with tears as he described those last moments. "I was camped with a group of Fitzhugh Lee's men. There were flags of truce placed all around. We all waited quietly outside the house where Lee and Grant were meeting to draw up the terms of surrender. When it was over, General Lee got on his faithful gray horse and rode our way. A bunch of us crowded around him as he came by. He paused briefly and said, 'I have done for you all that was in my power to do. You have done all your duty. Leave the result to God. Go to your homes and resume your occupations. Obey the laws and become good citizens as you were soldiers.' Then he rode away, staring straight ahead, his white hair uncovered and blowing in the wind. I'll never forget that moment or those words as long as I live."

I could feel the emotion in Conor's voice. Yet I couldn't help but think to myself, it was so like Conor to manage to be at that very place at that very time and be able to hear the farewell speech of our beloved general. Conor's sense of timing was always amazing.

When it was her turn, Olivia explained, "I didn't want to worry anyone when I realized that I was going to have a baby. Only your pa knew by way of the letter I had sent to him. I probably should have told all of you sooner. Things might have happened differently. The day Jessie and I found the letter you two boys left for us, we were beside ourselves. We were worried and sad, and then angry. We were glad you were going to help Nate, but we now had to fend for ourselves. Jessie and I decided we would get along just fine.

★ ★ ★

You two had gotten a few crops planted, such as they were, and Jessie and I managed to put away enough food to get us through the winter. When Jessie found out about the baby, she took it on herself to do the most demanding tasks so I wouldn't have to. The baby was born in December with Jessie by my side. Jessie wanted to name her Annie after her mother, and so we did. Thankfully Annie was healthy and strong. I don't know how I'd have managed without Jessie's help. We did what we needed to do to survive, but there were many things that were left undone. We were so glad to see Nate come home. He was finally able to meet his new baby daughter. And with him home we knew we were going to make it. Conor returned a short time after Nate. The only one missing was you. If you had been shot, neither Pa nor Conor had heard about it. But neither of them had seen you get captured either. So since April, we have been waitin' and wonderin' if we would ever see you again."

Then everyone listened as my turn came to relate all that had happened to me since that terrible day in April. I told them about being captured and sent to Point Lookout. But I didn't feel the need to tell them all the grim details of my three months of prison life. It was an unpleasantness I wanted to put behind me. I didn't want to burden them with those horrid scenes, either. Some things were best left to fade away like a bad dream.

As I sat surrounded by my loving family, I knew it was now time for our lives to move forward. We needed to start repairing the physical damage to our farm: mend the broken fences, restore the house, and work the land once more. It would be much more difficult though to mend our wounded

★ ★ ★

spirits and injured pride. Hard feelings can take a very long time to heal. Yet, I know we must look forward. There must be no more looking back.

Author's note: Point Lookout Prison was finally closed on July 13, 1865 by special order #168.

★ ★ ★

MAP 1861–1865

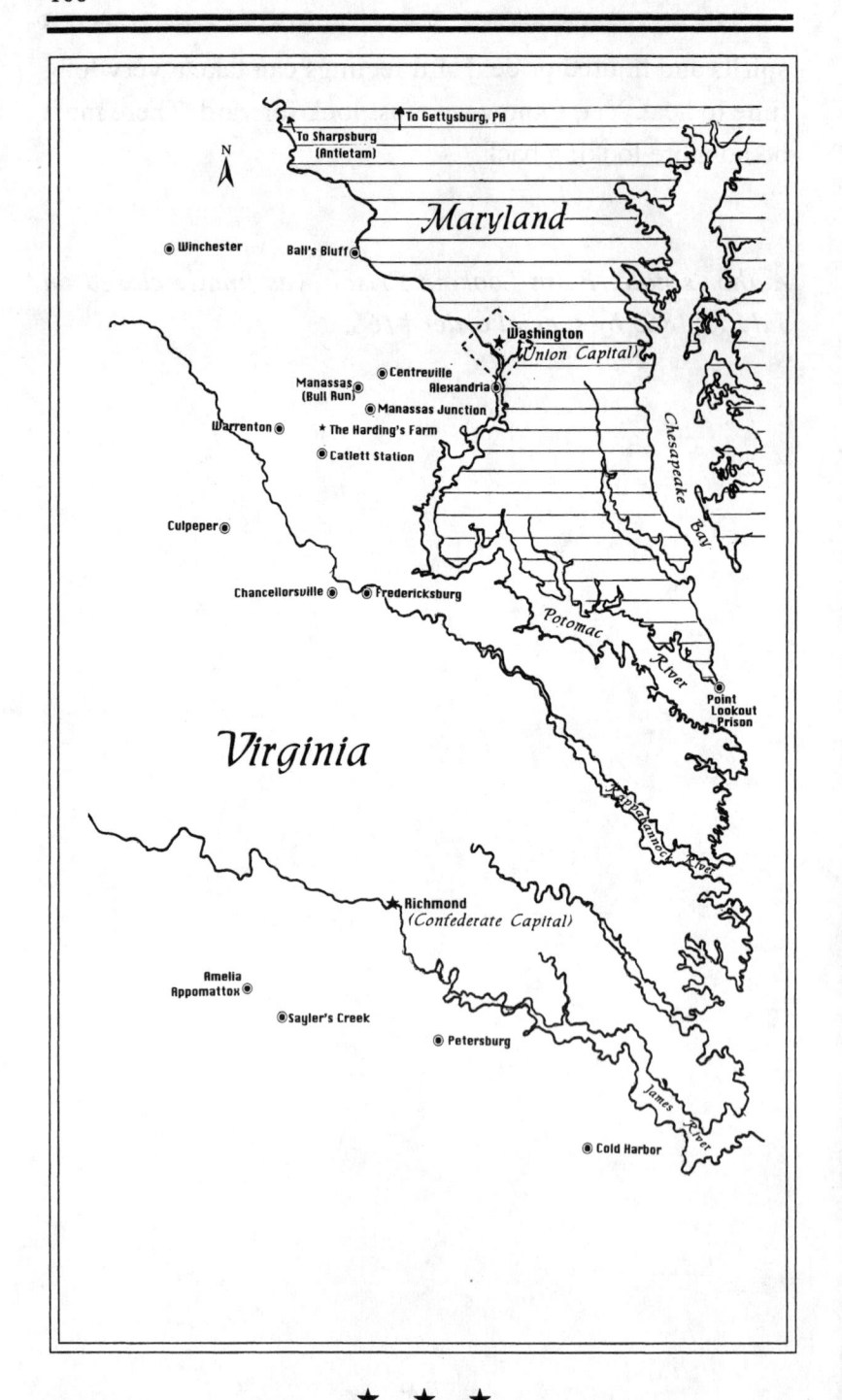

About the Author

Geraldine (Jeri) Susi has only to look out any one of her many windows in Catlett, Virginia, to view the settings for her historical stories. Surrounded by large horse and dairy farms, her home is nestled deep in the woods, with a babbling brook and a lily pond filled with goldfish. For many years, while Mrs. Susi was a reading teacher in Fairfax County, she drove through the Battlefield at Manassas (Bull Run), on her way to and from work. It was during this daily commute that her Civil War adventures came to life in her mind. Mrs. Susi experiences first hand every place that she includes in her stories. She takes great delight in sharing her love of history and making it come to life for others.

Mrs. Susi has traveled extensively all her life. She has been to every state in the United States and has lived in eight of them. She enjoys many hobbies including sewing, stained glass, and gardening, as well as bicycling and skiing.

Mrs. Susi and her husband, Ron, a retired Air Force pilot, have four grown children. Much to their delight, Mrs. Susi uses the names of her grandchildren for many of the fictional characters in her adventures.

A SERIES OF CIVIL WAR BOOKS FOR YOUNG READERS
by Geraldine Lee Susi

First in the series is *LOOKING FOR PA: A CIVIL WAR JOURNEY FROM CATLETT TO MANASSAS, 1861*. The book tells the tale of the Harding family struggling to endure the hardships of the Civil War as its violence, turmoil, and sacrifices forever change their peaceful existence in rural Virginia.

Young Jacob and Jessie Harding watch their father ride off to join the Confederate army, only to lose their mother to pneumonia six weeks later. They decide to go looking for Pa, and take Nanny, their goat, Squealer, their pig, and Cat with them. Traveling through the countryside, the determined little band encounters a wicked old man, a raging flood, a fierce mother bear protecting her cub, and a kindly freedman. They wind up at Bull Run near Manassas. It is on the battlefield that Jacob finds Pa, only to see him fall to a Yankee bullet. How the brave lad saves his father's life makes a touching and rewarding end to this true-to-life story.

LOOKING FOR PA is available in bookstores and from E.M. Press, Inc., P.O. Box 336, Warrenton, VA 20118 (540-349-9958) at a cost of $10.95.

★ ★ ★

With the release of *LOOKING BACK*, Mrs. Susi has given readers Book Two in the series.

Due to be released in 2002 is the last installment in the Harding trilogy, *LOOKING THROUGH GREAT-GRANDMOTHER'S EYES: REFLECTIONS ON LIFE DURING THE CIVIL WAR*. It is now the 1940's, and Jessie Harding comes to the forefront to tell this final chapter of her family's saga to her great-granddaughter, Piper. She tells about her life during and after the Civil War, reminiscing about the many difficulties women faced when their men went off to fight for the Rebel cause. Piper listens attentively as her great-grandmother recalls how she, as a young girl, had to stay at home and help farm the fields, can and prepare food, spin yarn for clothing, even assist in the birth of her own step-sister! Piper's fears for herself and for her own father, who is a soldier fighting far away in World War II, are eased when she learns how her great-grandmother overcame so much adversity. With American patriotism at an all-time high, Jessie tells Piper about the very different and divided patriotism of her youth. Even though everyone in her family fought for the Confederacy, Jessie shares with her great-granddaughter how she chanced to meet and marry a young Yankee soldier, and how that decision divided her loving family.

Expect to see *LOOKING THROUGH GREAT-GRANDMOTHER'S EYES: REFLECTIONS ON LIFE DURING THE CIVIL WAR* in bookstores soon!

★ ★ ★

TEACHER'S GUIDES AVAILABLE

Geraldine Lee Susi has written a comprehensive guide for classroom teachers to accompany each of her novels. Utilizing skills and expertise amassed during her 25 years as a reading specialist at the elementary and junior high school levels, she has developed each 16-page guide to assist teachers in their instruction of her Civil War books for young readers. The guides contain vocabulary exercises and cross-curricular activities, as well as comprehension and discussion questions designed not only to impart historical information, but to encourage student empathy with those involved in America's greatest tragedy.

The guides may be purchased from bookstores or ordered from E.M. Press, P.O. Box 336, Warrenton, VA 20188, (540-349-9958) for $7.00 each. A free guide accompanies an order of 10 or more books when purchased through the publisher.